# Gurkha

GURKHA

**First edition. March 3, 2025.**

Copyright © 2025 Robert J. Brodey.

ISBN: 978-0994065551

Written by Robert J. Brodey.

.

# Dedication

To the mountain people of Nepal, who over the millennia came to flourish in the rugged majesty of the Himalayas. And to the many generations of Nepali, who joined the ranks of the British and Indian military in the hopes of making a better life for themselves and their families.

To my beautiful family and friends: travel is awesome, but you are my one and only home.

This book is also dedicated to the creative team of Mike Carter, Bob Thompson, Biren Gurung, and Romelle Espiritu, who truly helped shape this story from a mere seedling of an idea.

## Note to the Reader

Although many of the events depicted in this novel regarding the Gurkhas and their historical place in British conflicts are based on documented facts, any resemblance to real persons, living or dead, is entirely coincidental.

This book contains references to war, violence, and colonial racism, which some may find upsetting.

*GURKHA (gur-kuh) n.*

Nepalese warriors sworn to protect the world from demons [mythic]; A Nepalese soldier in the British or Indian army [contemporary].

\*

*"It is better to die than live a coward."*
Gurkha Motto

# CYCLE

# I

*Tug a vine and start a landslide*
Nepali Proverb

# GURKHA

# THE HIDDEN VALLEY, 1914

The British arrived in the valley unannounced. They moved below on horseback, arriving from their distant military encampment in Pokhara on the edge of Phewa Lake. Behind the lead horses, dozens of pack animals roped together in a long line trudged onward. The sun had risen hours ago but remained hidden behind the mammoth ridges with their jagged rows of stone teeth that consumed the morning sky.

Smoke drifted from a dozen rustic huts dotting the hillsides among the agricultural terraces, while strings of colourful prayer flags flapped on a steady breeze. And all around, touching the thin air of the heavens, stood the snow-blown summits of the Himalaya range.

On a lower terrace, an old farmer dressed in traditional grey linens, his head crowned by a cup-shaped topi hat, coaxed two oxen forward with a long stick as they dragged a wooden hoe through the rocky field. As he called and clicked at the lumbering beasts, something on the ground caught his attention. He bent low to get a closer look. There before him, as clear as day, he saw an unnaturally large bear paw, perhaps two feet wide, stamped in the ground. The farmer did not investigate further—he had seen enough already—and fled toward the village to raise the alarm.

Up above, on a modest plot of land, Devi stood by her mother's earthen hut, her dark eyes following with curiosity, as the old farmer abandoned his oxen down below. Then she glimpsed the slow movement of the procession coming up the valley. A crescent smile appeared on her lips. *Strangers were coming to her village*, she thought.

The teen with long hair as black as a raven's wing had never gone beyond the knotted tree upriver by the pasture, which was a two-hour journey on foot. Down river, she had once gone as far as the bell-shaped stupa, a dirt and rock burial mound, at the point where two rivers joined together to make thunder. There, she and her father had once saved a bleating sheep stuck among the rocks of the frothing waters.

That was the extent of the physical world she knew, though her imagination allowed her to see far beyond. Still, she craved to know more about life outside her valley.

She took off running, descending the dirt path on a mission. Along the way, she passed massive yaks that slowly chewed the cud as they watched her go by. She greeted each one by name: *Namaste Padma!* *Hello Kale! Good day Tara!* A few women peered from doorways obscured by the billowing smoke from indoor cooking fires. They all looked disapprovingly at Devi's effortless, almost joyful flight down the mountainside.

Up ahead, Anish, a bright-eyed boy of eleven or twelve, straddled a tree branch overhanging the trail. He enthusiastically waved at Devi but instantly tumbled, hitting the dirt at Devi's feet. She gently lifted Anish upright, dusted him off with a few brisk sweeps of her hand, and then set off again, following the pull of gravity to the valley floor and the exotic strangers who she imagined had arrived from a faraway land.

In the near distance, barefoot villagers cautiously gathered around the approaching horsemen at the edge of the village. At the centre of the arriving party was the royal Rana of Gorkha dressed in a cape and jeweled headdress and surrounded by an entourage of Nepalese servants and a dozen or more British officers and soldiers with rifles slung over their shoulders.

Another line of soldiers with sharpened bayonets mounted on their rifles marched alongside several horses that struggled up the path hauling cannons with wooden wheels strapped with metal rims. A young child fled the frightening sight.

Both the men and women of Devi's village wore their hair long, which caused an amused murmur among the British ranks. Captain Hughes, a Welsh officer in his early thirties, adjusted his thin rimmed glasses and greeted the motley gathering. "Namaste," he said. Several villagers warily pressed their hands together and bowed to Hughes, while Lieutenant Colonel Young, the most senior member of the

British command present, frowned at the gesture. After all, the Nepalese had to rise to meet the British, not the other way around.

Devi's running flight came to a halt at the edge of the gathering. Anish breathlessly trailed behind. When his mother caught sight of him, she grabbed hold of her boy, eyeing the British and their weapons suspiciously. "They steal children for their armies," she whispered to the other mothers. They all murmured with simmering discontent but remained outwardly cautious in face of the powerful royal entourage and their British guests.

Lieutenant Colonel Young surveyed the villagers with their lethal curved kukri knives strapped around their waists. He plucked at the well-oiled moustache underneath his bony nose, then cleared his throat and pronounced: "We need fit young men!"

His words were met with an uneasy grumble from the adults of the village. Anish's mother scowled at Devi. "Every time she shows up, she brings bad luck." Others nodded gravely in agreement.

Devi felt the disapproving looks but stood her ground, held in place by a giant stone of pride. "What news of the outside world?" she called out to the pale faces on horseback.

Captain Hughes smiled at her curiosity and pushed his glasses higher up on his nose before speaking. "Well, young friend, there is chatter of war breaking out in Europe–"

"Who is to believe such nonsense!" replied Lieutenant Colonel Young, testily. "Beyond the empire, Germany is Britain's biggest trading partner. Why would we shoot ourselves in the foot with such tomfoolery!"

With that, the Rana and Young, who remained mounted on their horses, pointed to the young village men they wanted, as if selecting cattle. In turn, each recruit joined the entourage, some voluntarily, others by the forceful hand of the Rana's men. Corporal Smith, his face as flat and featureless as a plate, handed them some basic equipment, including a flask for water and a few cans of food. Each recruit received a silver coin for his troubles.

"You shall follow the horses on foot, you shall," Smith advised, in a posh accent that attempted to cover over his more humble Manchester roots.

Tension grew among the villagers, as their young men were being gathered. An elder reached for a rock on the ground, prepared to chase away the marauding outsiders with a hail of stones.

"We can't fight the warrior army of Gorkha," cautioned a voice from behind. "They will slay us all."

Grudgingly, the old man dropped the stone.

Just then Lieutenant Anwyl caught up with the rest of the hunting party. He was sweating, his posture slack, but trying to stand upright at attention. The lieutenant colonel eyed the lowly Welshman. "Must we wait for you all day, Taffy?" scolded Young. "Come on, then. The animals will all be dead of old age by the time our hunt gets underway!"

As the final selections were made, Young pointed his riding crop at the bright-eyed boy, Anish. He tried to step forward, to break from his mother's grasp, but she wouldn't let him go. Again, he twisted and turned to escape her grip, but her arms were forged from the rugged land itself, and Anish simply didn't have the strength to break free.

The Rana turned to one of his servants. "Bring some village girls to my tent tonight," he ordered.

The elder who had gripped the stone moments before heard this. "Hide the children," he whispered to the others. "ALL the children."

Captain Hughes could see the adults of the village growing agitated. "My friends," he said, disarmingly. "We didn't come to Nepal to steal." He raised his rifle. "We came to hunt!"

"For Mahisha?" asked Devi.

"Mahisha? What's a Mahisha?" queried Young. "Big game, I wonder?"

"The biggest," yelled the boy, Anish.

There was uneasy laughter from the villagers.

The Rana looked irritated and embarrassed. "Superstitious talk. By backward mountain goats!"

Devi pushed to the front of the small crowd and came face to face with the Rana and the British officers. "Mahisha is an *asura*! A demon!"

The hunting party laughed outright. All but Captain Hughes, who looked at her with questioning eyes. He moved to speak but was interrupted by Young. "What gibberish do these people speak of?"

"We speak the truth, *long nose*!" Devi called back.

Young tapped his nose. "This, you rascal, is an aristocratic nose! Bred through a pure line of blue blood for at least 500 years!"

Birendra, a villager with a scar across his forehead, hissed at Devi: "Always out to embarrass us, aren't you! Go home. Your mother needs you."

Devi paused on his words, then spoke. "I know my destiny. And it isn't washing clothes and hunting for firewood." With that, she stomped away. But only a few steps up the hill, she came upon the slow-moving farmer with the topi hat. "Run ahead," he gasped. "Warn the villagers. The demon is back! And he's bigger than ever!"

Devi wanted to help, to stop Mahisha and his trail of destruction. But it was no use. No one listened to her, anyway. She held out a hand, palm forward, and rattled her wrist in a gesture of refusal.

He looked at her in disbelief. "You are nothing like your father," he sputtered, toothlessly.

"Well, no one ever dared treat my father the way you all treat me now!"

He gave her a wary sidelong glance and hobbled onward to warn the others that the monster was amongst them once again.

*

A horse tethered with a rope grazed near the edge of Devi's family field, forest and shrub rising up beyond like a thick cloak. Devi moodily kneeled in the dirt, her sleeves rolled up, her muscular arms flexing as she grunted and pried a root from the earth with an old, rusted kukri knife.

Steps away, Devi's mother bent low and planted the field, humming. She was dressed like all widows—in a plain white shawl and a long white skirt. Her ear lobes, neck, and wrists where jewelry once hung when her husband was alive were now barren of glittering wealth. This absence was not lost on Devi.

The teen glanced over at the stone shed partly concealed by shrubs, where she and her mother stayed, sleeping on the dirt floor, when they had their periods. During this time, the rules of *chhaupadi* forbid them from entering the kitchen or taking part in religious functions or even bathing, because their menstrual blood was deemed impure.

"Is there a time when the thick rope of tradition you always talk about should be cut?" asked Devi.

A smile from her mother.

"What?"

"Ever since you were a little girl, you asked questions no other mouth spoke. Like you had eyes in the heavens looking down on us all."

Devi couldn't stay frustrated and fondly looked up at her mother. Then concern coloured the girl's expression. "I think the demon has returned to the valley."

"Our world is interwoven with that of gods and demons." Her mother smiled again, admiring her daughter. "We will deal with whatever comes our way, as we always have. As a family."

"Mama," Devi finally said. "Why do you always smile? Especially when the world can be such a terrible place."

Her mom tilted her head, acknowledging Devi's words. "You don't always have to smile because something makes you happy. Sometimes you can't wait for happiness to visit you, so you make it yourself, inviting it in with a smile, even when the universe only seems to offer up spoiled yak's milk."

She regarded Devi a long while, before speaking with an air approaching regret: "You know, I always thought things would be different for you."

"Ama-jee. Please."

"But things rarely work out."

"Papa may be gone. But I still have you."

Her mother sadly touched her bare wrist.

"One day I'll get your jewelry back," Devi promised.

"Oh, Devi. It was all meant for you. I'm sorry I had to sell it."

"I would trade all the gold bangles in the world to have *bubah* back with us."

"Perhaps in another time. Another place. You could have…"

"It's not your fault. It's mine." Devi bowed her head. "I bring bad luck."

"That's not true, Devi. You've been my greatest luck of all."

A tear buried deep within found its way to the surface and streaked down Devi's cheek, but she immediately hid her face from her mother's gaze.

"Never hide your tears. They contain all the love and healing in the world." Her mother approached and swept Devi's hair from her face. She smiled once again, as if returning to happier, more hopeful times before her husband had been killed. "One day you'll be worshipped like a goddess. And all the boys will stumble over each other to get near you. 'I want to marry her.' 'No, I do!'"

Just beyond sight, a rustling from the forest. But only the horse sensed the malevolent presence. It neighed and circled nervously, its head raised, ears angled back, on high alert.

"I'll never leave you," said Devi.

"Of course, you will! I want you to have a life." She pointed toward the forest and the mountains rising beyond. "The whole world is waiting for you!"

Devi concealed a toothy grin with a hand.

"My little girl, you could be such a devil! No wonder your father would call you Kali, the destroyer of illusions!"

There was more rustling from the edge of the forest, but Devi and her mother didn't hear it, too caught up in their moment together.

"But to me," continued her mom, "you're all the gods in one perfect daughter. That's why I named you Devi, after the Supreme Goddess..." Devi's mother clutched her stomach, lovingly.

"...Who holds the entire universe in her womb!" said Devi, completing her mother's sentence.

Her mother grinned then surveyed Devi's clothes. "Now we're really going to have to do something about these. You can't spend your whole life in boys' clothes! Especially if we're to find you a nice husband."

"Me get married? I'd rather collect firewood for the whole village—for the rest of my life!"

Together, they laughed, and time itself stood still. There was no past and no future. Only Devi and her mother in the field, their laughter defying their lot in life.

"Tonight, for dinner, I will make your favourite," said her mother, almost in song.

"*Dhido* and *gundruk ko zhol*!"

"A celebration of love!"

Deep animal growls came from the thick of the forest, rumbling underfoot like an earth tremor.

Wild-eyed with nostrils flared, Devi's horse broke loose from its tethering and bolted into the woods, while the birds in the trees took flight. The horse's shrill cry wiped the joy from Devi and her mother's face.

Devi felt her skin prickle, as she tried to make sense of what was happening.

"*NOW!*" commanded a rumbling voice from the forest.

13

A beast's claw released its grip on leashes made of bloody intestines, letting loose a pack of fanged demon dogs with white bulging eyes. Devi's mother pulled her behind and snatched up a rock from the ground. The demon dogs lunged at her. She thrashed the hairless beasts with the sharp edge of the rock, as they gnawed and tore at her flesh.

Devi remained frozen, shocked.

"Run, Devi!" cried her mom, who was quickly losing the battle against the soulless demon dogs.

A creature snatched Devi's mother up in its mighty jaws. Armed with the kukri knife, Devi leapt to her feet and faced off with the dog, its pink muscles glistening, veins bulging. Then, before Devi could take a slice out of the beast, it darted toward the cover of the forest.

"Ama!" cried Devi.

# LOST

Devi sprinted after the devilish creature that clutched her mother in its jaws. If she caught the demon, there was still a chance she could save her mother so that they could live out a simple life together.

Her eyes stayed fixed on the beast. The unearthly animal's thick muscular legs coiled and propelled it at tremendous speeds, forcing Devi to dig deep to keep it in her sights. It was the largest monster she had ever seen, but she pushed down her fears of the fight should she catch it.

Only when she glanced back did she see that her problems were not just in front of her, but also right behind. Half a dozen demon dogs chased after her. But she ran faster, determined, leaping a stream and darting and weaving between trees, using them as shields against the dogs snapping at her heels.

Devi ran for countless minutes, but still her mother lay ahead just out of reach, while the dogs threatened to overtake her from behind. As she turned toward her mother hanging limp in the demon's jaw, she stumbled over the uneven terrain and hit the ground. The dogs were upon her, but Devi jumped back to her feet and sprinted on.

The pursuing dogs split off in an attempt to flank her. The creature with her mother sped further ahead. Devi sprang, closing the enormous gap, the kukri outstretched. "Ama-jee!" she cried.

With the point of the kukri, she pegged the demon's tail to the ground. It howled like death itself. Devi reached for her mother, reaching for the only thing she had left to live for. Her mother's eyes sprang open in a burst of consciousness. "Run away while you can, Devi."

"No, mama!"

"I'm sorry..." she gasped. "...That I couldn't protect you..."

More dogs from the demon world leapt on Devi from all sides, snatching her hands and feet, dragging her away. But she responded with animal ferocity, thrashing and using her hands and feet to ward off the ghastly creatures. She reached out for her mother, but a dog bound on her back, its claws sinking into her flesh. She fought her way from beneath it and, defying nature, flung herself ten feet up to a branch overhead.

Crouched on the forest floor, an old man wearing a painted shaman's mask tracked her movement up. Hooked over his shoulder was a bamboo bow. A leather pouch contained a dozen arrows with fletchings of iridescent feathers. Strapped to his waist hung a sheathed kukri knife with an ornate handle made from a piece of ivory severed from the god Ganesh's tusk.

Devi balanced precariously on the branch, which groaned and bent with her weight. Down below, the vicious jaws of the demons snapped and frothed with anticipation. With a sharp crack, the branch gave way, and she crashed to the ground. The dogs didn't hesitate and pounced on her. But a quick succession of flaming arrows nailed the demon dogs. In the eye. Throat. Heart. The dogs bubbled and melted into pools of sulfurous liquid.

Devi raced toward her mother, but the demonic dog gnawed off its own tail, snatched up her mother, and darted off.

The girl watched helplessly, as the *asura* sped on toward Mahisha's kingdom of blackened stone perched below a mountain summit.

"Ama," whispered Devi.

Still wearing his shaman's mask, the old man approached. Devi's body tensed, in shock. *What kind of god or demon stood before her?* she wondered. Then her knees buckled, and she crumpled to the ground, unconscious.

*

An ethereal blue light clung to the forest, as sounds echoed—croaking frogs, clicking insects, and the wind passing through the leaves on the high tree branches. From the distant reaches of the wilderness, Saras-vati, the Hindu goddess of knowledge, art, and wisdom glowed like a lantern and played a gentle song on a pear-shaped veena with a long neck.

Still masked, the old man kneeled by a crackling fire. He hummed the tune being played by the goddess, as if his ear was tuned to another world, another plane of existence. He hovered over Devi, who remained unconscious, as he applied a paste to her tattered limbs.

In a dream, Devi was back at her village, sitting around a table on the ground with her mother and father in the flickering candlelight. Outside, the rain lashed her home. Bright flashes of lightning illuminated the world beyond the windows. Inside, her father was laughing as he told a story about a yak stealing his lunch, while he worked the fields.

A rumbling sound.

As it grew to a deafening roar, Devi and her parents looked to one another with wide eyes. *An earthquake? A—?*

The walls collapsed in on them, and the landslide swept away the table, the candlestick, the food and bowls, and her mother and father.

Devi awoke with a gasp, her vision filled with the menacing shaman's mask.

"Do not fear the mask," the man said, seeing the child's frightened eyes. He didn't hesitate and removed the mask, revealing his old-bearded face. "I am Dharma."

Devi couldn't respond, and for a long while, the girl with raven-black hair rocked back and forth by the fire, lost in memory, lost in sorrow. She thought about the death of her father, swallowed whole by the cruel monster, Mahisha, and her mother's own terrible treatment by the village, as if she had killed the man she loved. The terrible vision of her mother being carried away by the demon dog tore at Devi until she thought she would die.

On the other side of the flame, Dharma used his kukri knife to carve up a rodent he had caught. Dharma's movements were fluid, quick, and precise. The knife magically seemed to cut without making contact. He placed the meat on the fire, which sizzled in the open flames, fed by the animal's dripping fat.

He gazed at Devi inquiringly through the fire, the heat distorting her face. The old man passed Devi a piece of meat. "Eat, young man," he said.

Devi was too exhausted to correct the stranger.

*

It was morning and the sun fought its way through the mist. Several fish hung from a branch, freshly plucked from a nearby stream by Dharma. Devi remained fast asleep beside the dying embers of the campfire, while Dharma studied her arms and feet with great interest. Incredibly, there were no wounds. The lacerations left by the vicious demons had magically healed overnight.

As Devi stirred, Dharma rose to his feet and headed toward the woods. She immediately grew tense, not yet ready to be alone.

"Mahisha and his army have no interest in fish," he consoled, before disappearing into the thick foliage.

Devi poked the glowing embers with a stick then rested her head on her knees. She felt lost, unsure of who she was and what to do next. So she stayed in place, hoping the answers would come to her.

In the near distance, there was a sudden sound of crackling branches. She looked around, alarmed. "Dharma?"

But it wasn't the old man who approached—but rather a bear lumbering toward the fish hanging from the branch.

Devi drew her kukri and took large swipes at the approaching bear, but she was no match for this great hunter and forager.

"You killed my parents!" she cried, as she attacked with all her fury.

The bear, with its mighty paw, swatted her, sending her reeling. Devi regained her footing and instead of fleeing raged at the bear.

The furry beast bowled her over, knocking the wind out of her. She remained on the ground, trying to recover. It roared and pounced, its massive teeth threatening to swallow her up. From the corner of her eye, she saw Dharma reappear. "I thought you said Mahisha didn't like fish!"

Dharma drew his kukri and struck the bear down with a single stroke. As the bear toppled, Devi rolled out of the way, but her leg got trapped beneath.

"You killed the demon!" she said, as she tugged her leg free of the monster's dead weight.

"Don't be blinded by revenge," he said, impatiently. "Where you see an *asura*, there is only an animal of the forest. Next time I won't save you."

Devi now saw that she had erred. That she had, indeed, mistook a bear for Mahisha. "Teach me to fight."

"I'm afraid you are too full of anger. You are, it seems, your pain, which will dominate your every action, your every thought. It will sabotage then destroy you, if you don't respect it."

"I can block it out!"

Dharma could see that what the child wanted the child was not yet ready to receive. "You must learn to listen."

Devi studied him long and hard and whispered, "I will."

The old man straightened up, wiped clean the blood from the blade, and replaced it in its scabbard.

Devi couldn't conceal her disappointment.

But Dharma ignored her sullen expression and got down to the business of skinning the bear, slicing it up, and smoking the meat over the fire.

Throughout the day, Devi's anxiety grew, as she sat on her haunches, watching Dharma work, as if she wasn't there at all. She chopped listlessly at the dirt with her kukri, until she saw the old, bearded man approach the smoldering fire that had grown weak and kicked dirt over it, choking it until it was completely extinguished.

"Take me with you," she pleaded.

Dharma felt a pain in his gut from her words, but he blocked it out.
"I have nothing," she pleaded.

"Young man. Let me ask you something."

Devi gestured for him to proceed.

"Did your parents love you?"

"Yes," she nodded.

"Did they demonstrate their love and devotion?"

"Every chance they had. In the morning. In the field, while we worked. And even while I slept, I sometimes heard their praise and adoration."

"So very fortunate," he said, satisfied. "Then you know who you are. And you will be fine, even if this time of loss seems beyond your grasp to overcome."

That wasn't good enough for Devi, and a sinking feeling set in the pit of her stomach. She wanted to insist again, but she could see Dharma was ignoring her, busying himself packing the bear skin and the dried meat into a basket.

"There is plenty of meat left for your journey back to your village," he said, pointing to a length of fabric filled with cured meat that could be strapped around her shoulders.

"The demon killed everyone I loved. Do you understand? To my village, I'm dead. Worse than dead, even. They say I've brought them nothing but bad luck. And maybe I have. But leaving me now is the same as killing me."

Dharma avoided Devi's pleading gaze, as he readied his basket filled with meat and fish.

"I'm not a child. I can help you in your old age!"

She watched him, waiting, hopeful he would have a change of heart. He hoisted the basket onto his back and fastened it to his forehead with a thick strap. "I'm afraid you aren't welcome to come with me."

"I wish I had never known love," she blurted. "Having then losing is worse than never having at all."

"At least you have known love once," he said. "That's more than many will experience in a lifetime." With a thick, earth-stained hand, he pointed behind him. "I believe your village is somewhere back that way. Perhaps you can convince them of your good fortune with all this meat." With that, he walked off into the forest.

Devi remained in place, staring at the forest where the old man had departed, waiting for him to return. At any moment now, he would call back to invite her along. She was absolutely sure of it. But he did not. After countless minutes, a feeling like ice took over her body. She bumped the hefty load of meat wrapped in fabric onto her shoulders.

"Maybe I don't need you, after all," she called out in Dharma's direction, her fists clenched tight in angry balls. Then she hiked off in the opposite direction.

# DHARMA

On the valley floor, the Gorkha royal entourage and its British guests that Devi had spotted from her perch the previous day set up camp on the banks of a broad churning river. The riverbank was strewn with impossibly large boulders torn loose by frequent floods, making the encampment's canvas tents look like children's playthings.

At the centre of the camp was a large dining tent with several long tables and carpeted floors reserved for the Royal Rana and the senior British staff. A similar sized tent with dirt floors and rickety tables sat at the margins of the site and was meant for the lower ranks of the British military. Beyond the fringe dwelled the Nepalese servants, who lived and ate in a makeshift encampment, working and sleeping bunched together in tattered canvas shelters.

A tall wooden rack had been erected and strung with the latest kills from the hunting expedition, including several male bharals with large thick horns shaped like the curved blades of kukri knives.

By the banks of the river, a group of Welsh soldiers were laughing as they bantered, washed clothes, and cleaned their weapons. Lieutenant Anwyl was propped against a rock, reading *The Ancien Régime and the Revolution* by Alexis de Tocqueville, a small stack of books by his side like loyal companions. Private Hardie, who looked like he had just gotten out of bed with his tired eyes and sagging face, teased the lieutenant, despite his higher rank. "*Bois bach*, this is the army, not a library."

"I like to read, I do," offered Anwyl.

"Really?" replied Hardie. "If you hadn't told me, I wouldn't have been the wiser."

"Truly?"

"No, numbskull."

"The lieutenant likes his books so much, I've seen him in the shitter with 'em," added Private Cadogan, surveying the scene with his penetrating blue eyes.

Private Maddocks, with his mop of black hair, stood tall among the ranks of the Welsh. "Well, at least Anwyl's shits are smarter than them bloody dog-hearted English," he said, pointing to a small group of British troops huddled together around Corporal Smith, who was once again combing his hair smooth to his head.

"Ha, I reckon Anwyl's as Welsh as Swiss cheese," said another Welshman, still focused on teasing the easiest target in their ranks.

The lieutenant's small nervous frame made him the butt of jokes, and he knew that. Still, he never hesitated to fight back. "Well, my great grandfather marched with Frost and the Chartists on Westgate, he did."

"Go on, boy. The great rebellion clearly still beats in you," retorted Cadogan, before turning to the others. "He always gotta bring up Westgate. Because he's got no glory of his own!" He took a drink from his flask before looking at Anwyl with mock contempt. "Well, no matter. Ya drink like an English bastard, you do. Even my girlfriend could put you under the table."

"Bloody tidy, mun! The only licker Anwyl can hold is his tongue!" said Hardie. He proceeded to grab his own tongue and led himself around by it.

Among the band of British, Corporal Smith ceremoniously stood up, stripped down to his underwear, and waded into the river just upstream from a group of Nepalese servants, who were also bathing and washing their clothes.

As Corporal Smith soaped up, he looked to his mates then let loose a fountain of pee in the direction of the Nepalese downriver. "Filthy pygmies," he cursed, his Manchester accent thick on his tongue.

His men laughed, amused, while the Nepalese made muted gestures of protest, as they cleared out of the path of English piss.

"*Manchester*, you flat-faced bastard," shouted Maddocks. "Did your *tad* have sex with a plate to knit ya? Or did ya fall on your face as a filthy-assed baby *bachgen*?"

"Once again," Smith complained. "The inbred Welsh speaking their twisted tongue."

The Welsh soldiers found the attempted insult amusing, but their rising laughter was interrupted by Lieutenant Colonel Young, who approached through the boulder field. The Welshmen immediately got serious and busied themselves washing their clothes and cleaning their weapons.

"I see the coal miners stick together," sneered the lieutenant colonel. Then to Anwyl he added, "I would expect nothing less from you, lieutenant. Your short stature perfectly reflects your limited abilities."

"Well," said Anwyl, choking nervously on his own words. "Napolean says greatness is measured from the top of your head to the heavens—"

"Silence, you! In all my years as an officer, I've yet to meet a Welshman that lived up to his rank."

Maddocks, forever scowling, stepped forward to challenge his superior officer, but Cadogan knew better and pushed him back.

"The half-colonel is well deserving of a solid drubbing," Maddocks grumbled.

Young gave them one last look of contempt, awaited their salutes, then turned on his heels. "And get the bloody camp set already!" he shouted back.

"What'd I ever do to him?" sulked Anwyl.

Cadogan piped in, "You were born the wrong side of Bristol Channel, you were."

"Correction!" said Hardie. "Cardiff's the only side that counts!"

A rumble of approval.

"Low hanging fruit, if you ask me," growled Maddocks. "His words say more about his small mind than your height."

Anwyl broke off from the others and bent over the flowing river, splashing his face to cool off.

"So the lieutenant colonel is filling your ears with honey words?"

Anwyl looked back to see the friendly smile of Captain Hughes behind him. He saluted, then chirped, "Let him eat roast beef—sir."

The captain sighed. "The colonel has his ambitions like the rest of us. You've been here for what? Six weeks? I'll let you in on a little secret. If you only associate with your own kind, it makes it worse for all of us." Then, in a conciliatory manner, he added, "The way things work here in the Kingdom of Nepal is pretty much the same as home. We still take our orders from the English. Only now these hillmen sit a rung below us."

"Like the Paddies and Pikeys."

"Leave the Irish out of it," said Hughes, kindly. "My mother's line is pure Galway."

"My apologies, sir. I should know better." With that, Anwyl palmed water from the river to drink.

As Hughes turned away, he warned, "With all the men in the river, I don't recommend drinking here. Perhaps find a spot further up."

Anwyl was tired of being told what to do, so he drank, anyway.

\*

The old man, Dharma, spent the day trekking through the forest with his massive load of fish and bear meat. Every so often, he would look back to see if the strange boy with the fast-healing wounds was following him. He had his regrets leaving that poor child back there to fend for himself, but it was better to learn now that he was alone in the world, the old man reasoned, than to create a false sense of hope.

When night fell, Dharma didn't even light a fire and slept curled up in the protective arms of giant tree roots, his kukri knife, as always, close at hand. In the morning, his first thought was of the boy, and he imagined that by now the child was back at his village, receiving a hero's welcome with all the fresh meat tied to his back.

The old man hiked with swift short strides over the final slope that would lead him back to his village. Finally, after trotting down the far side of the ridge, he came upon the Kali Gandaki River. A suspended rope bridge spanned the river's thundering waters. He was grateful it remained intact. Every time the bridge was destroyed by storm or rumbling earthquake, it added days to the journey home.

He kneeled by the river's edge and drank water thirstily from the cup of his hands.

A sound.

Dharma turned swiftly and nearly toppled over. Beside him was the orphan-child with long hair, drinking with his head plunged under the water like an aquatic bird. The old man could barely believe his eyes. For more than a day, this teen had been following him home undetected like a phantasm. Dharma looked to the heavens with pleading eyes before the mysterious child emerged from the water, hair dripping.

With resignation, Dharma wordlessly returned to his feet and walked over the swinging bridge toward his village in the distance, where faint whiffs of cooking smoke rose from the houses surrounded by rice terraces. Devi followed right behind, absorbing her surroundings. Beyond the lower fold of mountains, she saw the source of all her sorrow—Mahisha's kingdom of blackened stone perched among the high mountains. Strung from its parapets were not the usual colourful prayer flags but rather singed black ones.

In time, the path veered away from the river and met with a thousand stone steps heading up through many levels of farming terraces. At the foot of the staircase, though, Devi and Dharma spotted the canvas tents of an encampment spread out along the riverbanks by the boulder field. She wordlessly looked to the old man for answers, but he had none. With a sigh, he began to climb the long staircase, doing his best to ignore the child. With kukri in hand, she practiced knife strikes, imagining Mahisha lay just beyond the point of her weapon and her mother was still alive and in need of rescue.

The steps broadened, passing a bamboo pipe that channeled water into a basin, where several women and children collected water in ceramic vessels. Devi could smell the wet dirt, her senses alight.

On a stone terrace, a silver-haired woman sat cross-legged and squinted against the sun, as she spun sheep's wool into yarn using a rudimentary device with a stone wheel and wooden crank. Behind her, lengths of freshly dyed fabrics of every imaginable colour hung on a line to dry.

Smoke rose from dozens of houses, while an elaborate Hindu temple crowned the hilltop. Several children flew paper kites that darted back and forth across the sky, while a man shouldered a long stick with heavy woven baskets balanced on both ends. Reclined beneath the shade of a tree, a gaunt young man with a wispy moustache straightened up when he saw Devi and tracked her movement across the plaza with suspicion.

Devi followed Dharma into the dusty plaza, her eyes darting this way and that trying to take in every new sight. The narrow laneways between the houses were alive with activity, while strings of chili pods hung in windows to dry in the sun. In the open square, a group of boys with short hair snaked their way playfully around the village elders. "Here, only girls have long hair," Dharma commented to Devi.

"But I am a—" she started to say, but an inquiring glance from Dharma shut her mouth tight.

Beneath an open canopy, an ironsmith forged a kukri over hot flames. Devi was fascinated by the hammering and flying sparks. "Did he make your kukri?"

Dharma preferred silence and had no interest being a guide for this stranger. He removed the basket from his back and placed it on the ground.

Devi absorbed her surroundings, watching a little girl cling to her father's leg as he walked. "Pukuli," the man said. "When I am old, this is how I want you to carry me around the village."

"*Bubah*, you are never going to grow old!" the little girl exclaimed.

Devi smiled inwardly, recognizing in the child a spark, a spirit that she saw in herself—at least before Mahisha had stolen it from her.

From a narrow alleyway between a row of stone houses, a mammoth Tibetan mastiff, with a thick black and auburn coat and drooping eyelids, trotted into view and came to Dharma's side, expecting to be petted. The old man obliged. Devi had never seen a dog that large and was about to pet it, when Dharma warned against it. "The Bhote is an intelligent creature and isn't easily fooled. It's also determined and very protective, so it might mistake your intentions, if you get too near *its people*. Let it get to know you first."

Dharma pulled out a slab of bear meat from his basket and fed it to the mastiff.

In that moment, Devi's attention was stolen by a handsome teenager, who was kneeling in front of a painting on the plaza wall of the supreme goddess, Devi, many handed, riding on the back of a tiger. In Nepali it was written beneath: DEVI, OUR PROTECTOR. He then placed an offering—a lotus flower—on the ground before the image of the Goddess. As he wiped his brow with a red and yellow kerchief, the young man noticed the group gathered around Dharma.

The young man stood and made his way toward Dharma, bowing to the elder. "May Lord Krishna bless you," he said.

"Blessings to you, Arjuna," replied Dharma.

As the teen looked up, he caught sight of Devi. He was immediately taken aback by her strong lean shoulders, dark penetrating eyes, and lips that remained sealed in perfect crescents.

Devi saw the young intriguing man staring at her but couldn't sustain the intensity of his gaze and looked away. Instead, she found herself nervously fidgeting with the handle of her kukri strapped to her waist.

A man with grey stubble and impeccable upright posture approached Dharma, his hands clasped behind his back. At his side was a youth with his chest cocked forward and arms puffed wide, as if trying to give the impression he was twice the size. He lacked good looks and brawn but still found reason to swagger. Those gathered bowed with joined palms and cleared the way respectfully for the man with the grey stubble.

"Dharma!" he called out. "You brought back quite the prize of meat," he said, brightly, of the basket of bear meat and fish now resting on the ground.

"If you only depend on others, you will soon go hungry," said Dharma, gravely.

"Thankfully, our village shares its wealth—amongst each other and with the gods—so we can only hope we shall never know an empty belly."

"*He who only cooks for himself, eats sin,*" affirmed Dharma.

"You do love quoting your *Bhagavad Gita,*" said the man with the grey stubble before turning to Devi with a kindly gaze. He pointed to Arjuna and the braggart. "Have you been introduced to my brave sons?" he asked of the new arrival.

"I'm Tej, the protector," boasted the one with the puffed chest. "When I blow onto the battlefield, I fan the flames of war!"

His father did not appear impressed by his older son's immodesty but said nothing.

Arjuna bowed silently to Devi.

"Who's the kid, Dharma?" asked Tej, pointing to Devi.

"A stranger...Passing through," is all the old man offered.

Devi felt the familiar sting of rejection but remained motionless. She would not and could not go home to her village, and she wasn't prepared to live in the mountains alone, foraging and hunting in solitude. Even before arriving in the square, she had decided that she would tolerate all forms of insult in this new village, if it meant she could stay.

Tej's younger brother, Arjuna, leaned in to inhale her fragrance. For an instant, he was lost in her scent. "What brings this fair goddess among us?" Arjuna asked.

The laughter was immediate and explosive, and Arjuna looked about confused, as his father and Tej doubled over hysterical. Even Dharma, forever stoic, could not contain a grin.

"You shame yourself," said Tej.

Arjuna's cheeks flushed, despite not knowing for what he should feel shame.

"The stranger is a *BOY!*" continued Tej.

"An honest mistake," said Dharma. "In the western valley, even men have long hair."

Devi stood in place, "My name is...Dev."

"See, Arjuna. Have you ever met a girl named Dev!"

Arjuna could bear it no longer and escaped the humiliation.

Arjuna's father turned to Devi. "My apologies, Dev. One day, he'll be a great warrior. Until then, we must humour him."

"Then I hope one day to fight Mahisha—with Arjuna by my side."

Arjuna's father tilted his head in approval.

Out of the corner of her eye, Devi noticed Captain Hughes and Lieutenant Colonel Young standing before a line of local men. *Long nose*, she murmured contemptuously in recognition. It must have been their tents below, she thought. Then she asked Dharma, "Are they here recruiting for their hunting expedition?"

"Why, they're recruiting Gurkhas, of course!" Tej piped in.

"Gurkhas?"

"From what star has this boy fallen?" asked Tej.

Arjuna's father offered an explanation. "Gurkhas are warriors. Forged by the gods. To protect the earth from the forces of darkness."

"And sometimes we give the British a hand..." said Tej, drawing and thrusting his kukri. "...with their DEMONS!"

Tej's father gestured impatiently for him to settle down. "A warrior must remain humble and forever in the service of what is right and good."

Across the busy plaza, Hughes caught sight of Devi and regarded her with interest. "Namaste," he said aloud to her, but not loud enough for her to hear at that distance.

"What's that even mean?" ask Corporal Smith, testily.

"*The Divine within me bows to the Divine within you,*" he responded, patiently. "Or simply, *I bow to you,* depending on the interpretation."

"Such rubbish, isn't it?" said Smith, with the muddled accent of one trying to jump stations in life by concealing the class he was born into.

Hughes ignored the junior officer and pointed to Devi. "Isn't that the child from the other village a few days back asking about life beyond the Himalaya?" His superior, Young, seemed annoyed by the question, but Hughes persisted: "She mentioned something about a Mahisha. Some kind of demon or whatnot."

"How in God's green earth should I know?" said the lieutenant colonel, impatiently, as he plucked at his oiled moustache. "They all look the bloody same to me. And what kind of fool would I be to believe in demons!"

From her place, Devi could see the officers looking in her direction, so she turned away quickly. Only then did she see Dharma lumbering out of the plaza. She quickly unburdened herself of the load of meat she had been carrying for so long. "Please," she said to the others gathered in the plaza. "A small gift."

As the villagers rushed to help themselves to the bounty, Devi quickly raced after Dharma. And in her haste, she didn't see Arjuna pressed against the wall, peering out angrily at the stranger, the source of his humiliation.

\*

That night, by candlelight, Captain Hughes was writing at a table inside a high-ceilinged tent, his fountain pen dancing over the page. The wooden table at which he worked was piled with books. As he wrote, pounding drums and crashing sounds from the village had him jumping from his seat, startled.

Private Cadogan cleared his throat to make his presence known then entered through the flaps.

"Captain Hughes, sir," he said, saluting.

"At ease, private." Hughes glanced outside. "What is all the racket, may I ask?"

"I believe kids are walkin' 'round the village with bells and drums and cymbals."

"What ever for?"

"To chase away the bad spirits and misfortune. Apparently, it happens a couple times a year." Cadogan hedged. "Sir, sorry to bother you."

"No bother at all."

"It's Anwyl. He's fallen sick, and he's in a bad way."

The captain put down his fountain pen and followed Cadogan's loping stride across their makeshift compound setup outside of Dharma's village. They entered a medical tent that hung heavy with the scent of human sickness and approached Anwyl, who was pale and shivering in a cot, his head haloed in sweat.

"Dr. Edward," said Hughes, greeting the doctor taking the sick man's temperature. "How's the lad doing?"

"Would they drink from the Taff River? No!" said the English doctor. "But for some foolish reason these Welsh boys think it's okay to drink this filth!"

"With all due respect," said Hughes. "I drink the water all the time. The Himalaya have some of the purest water in the world, melted straight from the glaciers."

Hughes could see the distain on the doctor's face and thought it prudent to finish with the conversation quickly. He pointed down to Anwyl in the cot. "I'll keep an eye on him. Thank you for your time."

The doctor gladly took his leave.

"Thank you, Captain," groaned Anwyl.

"Don't mention it."

"I mean thanks for getting rid of 'em. A bigger pain in the arse than the dysentery, he is. Pardon my French, sir." Anwyl felt deeply unwell, but he still managed to make himself laugh.

"Indeed." Hughes paused then ventured to ask, "If you didn't want to take commands from the English, well, why join the army?"

"Truly? I wanted to study paleontology. As a boy, I'd heard they'd found Neanderthals in Wales."

Captain Hughes cracked a smile. "Don't let the lieutenant colonel hear you say that. It'll only prove his point that we Welsh are backward apes. Once upon a time, I myself fancied becoming an anthropologist."

"As far as I can see, sir, it's just a matter of opportunity," Anwyl said, pointing to the stacks of books by his bedside. "In my village, you either go down the coal mines or join the British army. And I'm afraid of the dark—"

"So you learned to shoot a gun," said Hughes, finishing his sentence.

"Barely."

They shared a laugh, before Anwyl gagged and heaved into a pail set beside his bed.

The captain found a clean cloth, which he dipped in a basin of cool water and used to pat down the young man's face.

"Thank you, sir. You're too kind."

"Did I not warn you about drinking water from that part of the river?"

"You did, sir. And for that I apologize."

Hughes looked to Anwyl's stack of books. Among them was *War and Peace* and Tocqueville's book on the French Revolution.

Through his ill haze, Anwyl saw Hughes admire his collection of books, and it made him very happy. "The French Revolution. A Greek tragedy of modern times, it is."

"We humans can be a ghastly lot," offered Hughes.

"But to learn about our inner nature..." Anwyl took a moment to collect his thoughts, sweating and breathless, his eyes cast to the ceiling, as if seeking answers from beyond.

"Rest young man."

"Honestly, I don't understand this world, sir," said Anwyl, his thoughts feverish. "Life is this precious miracle. So why do we humans, then, always spoil it with our madness?" He paused, unable to hold up his head, as if terribly drunk. He wanted to go on but was cut short by a wet, gurgling cough.

Hughes hurried and fetched him a glass of water. "It's boiled," he assured him. Then he consoled the sick young man. "I'm afraid I can't answer your question, lieutenant. And in your current state, I suspect you aren't in a condition to answer, either." He wagged a finger at the stack of books. "Good reading is scarce in these parts. I hope you don't mind if I ask to borrow some of your books one day."

"O, it would be my honour, sir."

Hughes pulled up a chair beside Anwyl's bed. "Settle in now, lad."

Anwyl nodded, his body exhausted, his mind drifting off beyond conscious thought. Hughes leaned back in his chair and got as comfortable as he could on the unforgiving wooden seat. In the darkness beyond the tent, the clang of cymbals and the thump of drums from the village came in spasms, shattering the stillness and, Hughes imagined, chasing away the frightened spirits. And for the captain, too, there would be no sleep. For the rest of the night, he sat awake at his countryman's side until Anwyl's fever finally broke in the morning.

# OF DEMONS

From the darkness, the rustic room of Dharma's hut faded into view. Recessed into one wall, an oil lamp burned beside a small statue. This was an altar for pujas, offerings to the gods. Resting against the wall were different types of weapons—spears, swords, and bows and arrows. An iron pot sat over a fire, the smoke billowing out the open window and door. Devi's blurred vision fell upon the old, bearded man as he hunched over reading a book, the *Bhagavad Gita*. Several shaman's masks hung on the wall behind him, as if the spirits themselves dwelled within the walls of Dharma's abode.

Devi noticed an old wooden trunk sitting in the corner of the room. In faded paint, the side of the box read: *British East India Co.* It seemed an unusual possession for a hillman, and she wondered what mysteries it contained within.

When Dharma saw that Devi had stirred, he silently raised an empty pail for her to take. If she wanted to stay, Devi knew she would need to prove her worth, so she rose from her bed of straw and fetched the bucket from the elder's outstretched hand.

At the doorway, Devi admired the stone temple with its ornate pagoda roof on the opposite hill. Below, the rice terraces formed perfect arcs down the slopes. She yawned, stretching her arms wide, banging the pail with a clang against the doorway.

Dharma sighed heavily. Life was infinitely quieter alone, he thought.

Devi hiked down past terraces growing millet, rice, and short ears of corn. She was always happier to be outside, away from the confining walls of the indoors, absorbing the world around her. Huts dotted the hillside in a similar fashion to her own village, though these houses seemed larger and more finely finished, with smooth plaster walls and sculpted adornments at the entrances to keep the dark spirits away.

In the near distance, an elephant ridden by a man in a colourful topi hat struggled to free a stump from the ground. The man called sweetly but firmly to the beast, as its magnificent trunk curled tight like a fist around the stump, pulling and pulling until the earth finally yielded the dead tree with its spindly roots like the many arms of the goddess Kali.

Further down, Devi passed a woman marching uphill hauling a large bundle of firewood on her back. "Auntie, do you need a hand?" asked Devi.

"Thank you, my son. But this is a woman's work..."

Devi felt a pang in her chest. It was a feeling of guilt. A feeling that she was abandoning, if not betraying, the sisterhood that bound women and girls together. After all, she had only just declared herself a boy the previous day. And now the rules she would have to live by would be completely different.

When Devi arrived riverside, she placed down the empty pail and began moving in slow flowing circles, her hands shaped like sharp blades thrusting and warding off unseen foes.

The Hindu god, Shiva—blue and radiating light—sat on a branch of a tree with a damaru drum. The beautiful goddess Parvati lounged in the grass beneath, gazing up at Shiva. "My beloved Shiva," she called. "Dance another universe into creation for my amusement."

Shiva smiled, his teeth sparkling in a most magnificent white light. Parvati swooned, as he began to play his drum.

Devi drew her kukri from its sheath. "Dance another universe into creation," she repeated to herself, striking upward with the blade. As she moved, she felt her soul ache with the loss of her mother, an emptiness that threatened to swallow her. But then, in the darkness, she smiled, remembering how her mother always found reason to smile, no matter the situation. *Happiness isn't in things. It is in us.*

In the bushes, light and colour bent around the silhouette of the demon Mahisha's buffalo head, as he watched Devi across the river hacking and chopping with her kukri.

The sound of Shiva's drum sped up. Devi's bare feet kicked up dust as she spun and stepped like a dance, keeping time with Shiva's drum. Devi switched the kukri from her right to left hand then back again with seamless fluidity. The harder she worked, the broader she smiled. Even Shiva looked down from his branch, impressed.

"I heard music," said a voice from the bushes.

Devi spun around to see Dharma. She looked toward the tree, but Shiva and Parvati had vanished.

Dharma squatted by the river and patted the ground beside him in invitation. She joined him on the grass, expectantly. He took a deep meditative breath and spoke: "It was a mistake to follow me back."

"So I belong nowhere in this world."

"I didn't say that," he sighed.

A silence fell between them until Dharma confessed, "I raised an orphan—once. It didn't go well."

"But I'm different!" she pleaded. "I can help you."

Dharma wasn't certain he could persuade the child, so he changed the topic. "You never did tell me where home was."

"*Lukēkō Upatyakā.*"

"Hidden Valley," he repeated, curiously.

"What is it? Why do you look so amused?"

"Legend has it that it's a mythological place—occupied by *gods.*"

A black bird with a collar of white feathers landed nearby, dug into the dirt, and fished out a worm from a patch of grass layered with leaves. With the prize secured in its short beak, the bird took off once again.

Dharma regarded Devi observing the bird take flight. "Did you notice anything in particular?" he asked.

"The flapping wings made the leaves float away."

"Precisely. Everything influences everything. Even the smallest ripple on a pond can have great consequences for the world." He wagged his finger at her, pleased. "You are a good observer, Dev."

Devi bowed her head to conceal a smile.

"I saw you that day," he continued. "Battling Mahisha's beasts. You are a piece of iron. Not yet sharpened to a point."

Without hesitation, Devi rose to her feet. "Train me, and I'll leave forever."

Dharma raised a hand to quiet her momentary enthusiasm.

"I don't care about anything else. Do you understand? Not food. Not love. None of it matters any more. None of it! I just want Mahisha's blood."

"Renunciation alone doesn't bring enlightenment."

"Enlightenment? I don't care about enlightenment. I want revenge."

Dharma sighed loudly and gazed with great uncertainty at Devi's reflection shifting in the ever-changing surface of the river.

Then, with great seriousness, he stood and pointed around to the earth, trees, and sky above. "The source of life...," he said, tapping his heart. "...flows through here."

Dharma crouched low with kukri in hand and took a step forward before making an upward chopping motion with the knife. "Attack swiftly from below and strike upward, unifying heaven and earth."

Devi mimicked Dharma's every move with remarkable precision, though the old man could see she was holding her breath with concentration.

He demonstrated how to breathe properly so that she could stay energized and focused for long bouts of combat. "All the secrets of life live in the breath," he offered.

Again, Devi copied Dharma's inflow and outflow of breath, and she couldn't help but think she was impressing her teacher, but then the old man straightened up and sheathed his kukri in its scabbard. He pointed to the bucket on the ground.

"Fill it up so I can make some tea," he said.

Wordlessly, she watched him walk away.

*

For several weeks, Devi expected to be sent away from Dharma's hillside abode. She tried to push away that thought and what she would do when that time came. But each morning, he would point to the bucket and send her down to the river to fetch water. She used that time by the river to train, to get stronger. Her hunger for revenge dominated her every thought. Then, one morning, as she was filling the bucket with water, a voice called to her from the forest. Without hesitation, she entered, kukri drawn.

Further down stream, Tej and Arjuna bathed in the shallows of the river. Arjuna washed himself with his favourite red and yellow kerchief he had once traded with a traveller from the impossibly distant city of Kathmandu.

"I'm Tej, the bravest of the brave!" he boasted, with his usual hyperbole. "The protector who blows away his enemies!"

"Big brother," said Arjuna, kindly. "Who are you trying to convince? There's no one here but us."

"A fair question! I am merely reminding the gods that I am here to defend the mortals down below!"

Arjuna had known his brother all his life and had never known him *not* to brag. But his brother did have admirable traits—like his fierce loyalty.

Nearby, Devi backed out of the forest into the clearing, crouched low, kukri in hand.

A ragged bear emerged from the bush, swiping at Devi.

Arjuna moved to stand, but Tej held him in his place, grinning. He wanted to see what this stranger was capable of in battle before intervening.

Devi weaved in and out, avoiding the bear's claws, breathing steadily, as Dharma had taught her. She dove between the bear's legs and popped up behind. Confounded, the tattered bear looked about, seeking her. Devi didn't hesitate and lunged onto the bear's back, riding it like a mythical being.

For Arjuna and Tej, it was an incredible sight, and they both watched slack-jawed.

With determination, Devi struck, as the bear whirled and whirled in circles, the knife missing its mark each time. She struck again, and this time the bear dislodged Devi and tossed her to the ground. The bear pounced, pinning her down. Devi remained trapped and shouted at the bear in frustration.

"Clear your mind of all thought," said the bear.

Arjuna and Tej could not blink or move, as they heard the animal talk to Devi.

No sooner had the bear spoken did it throw off its tattered fur, revealing the old man, Dharma. "Let duty and not anger guide your blade," he advised.

Arjuna looked to his brother with a furrowed brow. "Why is Dharma training a total stranger when he says he's too old to train us?"

"There, there, Arjuna. Don't be jealous of the new kid."

"I'm not."

"I know you thought Dev was a *fair goddess*, but he's actually a decent warrior. If Dharma won't train you, I will. I already know everything I need to know."

Arjuna watched as Dharma jumped to his feet, brandishing the kukri. Devi faced off with her knife, hungry for more.

"Your confidence must not be grounded in how the battle is going but instead on your total commitment to each and every movement.

By making every action," Dharma said, slashing and thrusting, "precise, powerful, and fatal, your enemies will truly have something to fear."

Devi regarded him seriously.

"And you must practice, practice, practice."

"I'll learn," she declared.

"Learn to remember. Practice to forget." Dharma replaced his knife in its scabbard and headed toward the forest.

Before he disappeared into the woods, he called back to Devi, "And fill that bucket so I can make some tea!"

Devi looked toward the river and saw Tej and Arjuna sitting chest deep in water. She ducked behind a tree, covertly watching Arjuna. Devi's face softened, as she allowed herself to admire what she saw. His dark eyes seemed as deep and mysterious as that of a cave, while his serene face seemed to mask a great seriousness. Her eyes moved lower to his muscular body that appeared to have been carved from the same stone as the Himalayas.

"Join us!" called Tej, who stood, nearly naked but for a loin cloth. Seated in the water, Arjuna studied her with intrigue and uncertainty. *How could such a young man possess such...charisma*, he thought. He dared not think of the word *attraction* in the same breath as the stranger.

Devi backed away from the naked man. "Stay where you are! I...I'm off to hunt the demon."

Tej shamelessly marched toward Devi. "We've lived a long time in his shadow. The beast is seen only when he wants to be seen."

Devi's cheeks flushed, and she looked away from his nakedness, which was not lost on Arjuna.

Tej puffed his chest. "Besides, these days the British choose our battles." Tej paused a second then his posture slackened. "Dharma says Mahisha killed your parents. Is that true?"

Devi bowed her head. "My mother sacrificed everything to protect me. That's the kind of woman she was. But I couldn't protect her."

Tej nodded, thoughtfully.

"Don't even think about it, Tej," said Arjuna.

"Perhaps we've waited long enough for that beast to make a move. Maybe it's time I slay the *asura* myself."

"Don't be foolish!" Arjuna chastised.

Tej slipped on his clothes and handed Devi his sheathed kukri with the spiral design on the handle. "Only a real god can slay Mahisha with these," he said mischievously, wriggling his fingers.

"A warrior should never be separated from his kukri," she cautioned.

Tej stepped back with a wink. "Leave the worrying to Arjuna!" With exaggerated stealth, Tej bound into the forest.

Arjuna turned to Devi, annoyed with the stranger. "You're going to get him killed."

She wanted to protest but said nothing.

*

Out front of Dharma's stone house, the old man sat on a flat rock in his field, legs crossed, with hands folded in his lap. His breath was deep and slow like that of a dying man. His eyes were closed against the world, and he focused on the darkness of his closed eyelids, seeing patterns and shapes float back and forth across the abyss of his mind. He remained deep inside his breath for countless minutes, and it was only as he emerged from a deep state of meditation that the stranger with long black hair and penetrating eyes appeared in his mind's eye once again. The child with unique physical gifts had only been with him a short time but had already made a deep impression.

As if echoing the projections of his mind, Devi emerged into the clearing. In one hand, she clutched Tej's kukri with the spiral handle. With the other, she held up the pail filled with water. "Now you can make your tea," she offered.

Dharma glanced toward Mahisha's kingdom nestled into the head-wall of a mighty summit. A yellow haze clung to the stone fortress walls, the blackened prayer flags flapping. In the distance, a clear line existed between the green fertile land and the burnt smoldering fields leading down from Mahisha's stronghold. The old man stroked his beard, deep in thought. As of late, there had been unprecedented developments at the demon's lair with more and more land consumed by fire and his towers soaring ever higher. His powers seemed only to grow, as if feeding off the rising chaos and discord of the human world. Dharma couldn't help but think that perhaps the stranger had somehow unsettled the tenuous balance between Mahisha and the people of the lower valleys.

"Everyone has strengths and weaknesses. Even gods and demons," said Dharma, finally.

Devi regarded the old man, who did not meet eyes with her. "How do I destroy him?"

"Destroy? Nothing can be destroyed." Dharma made a circle in the sky. "Energy flows, changing like the seasons. Without end. To prevail you must embrace him like someone you love."

At that moment, Arjuna walked into view down below. Devi suppressed a smile. Then something rustled in the bushes, and Devi spun toward the forest gripping a knife in each hand. A foraging large-eared pika sprung from the underbrush, and the tension in her posture immediately broke.

That's when a large tremor jolted them like an earthquake.

As Devi and Dharma sought the source of the disturbance, they caught sight of Tej entering the clearing along a rice terrace below. Behind him rose Mahisha on hind legs, bear-like with wild tufts of hair. A rounded belly hinted at his insatiable appetite. Set into his mammoth head and protruding frontal lobe were a pair of small close-set eyes. Around him, light bent, distorting everything.

Arjuna, who was still some distance away, saw his brother in immediate danger and shouted, "T-E-J-J-J-J-J!!"

Tej heard nothing, too deep in thought of his own grandeur. Only when there was a subtle change in light did he turn to see that the growing shadow being cast belonged to the other-worldly beast, Mahisha. He reached for his belt only to remember he had given his knife to the stranger for safe keeping. For his own foolish vanity.

Devi looked down at Tej's kukri in hand and bolted, but Dharma clipped her feet, sending her tumbling. Both kukris slipped from her grasp, disappearing into the underbrush. "You're not ready," Dharma said, before racing down the hill toward Mahisha and Tej.

Frantically, Devi scrambled in search of the kukris in the tall grass. She looked up and saw Tej being smashed by the demon. He tumbled and splayed on the ground, winded, but he bravely staggered to his feet only to be met by Mahisha's slashing claws, leaving bloody marks across his chest. The devilish *asura* spotted Devi on the hilltop and grinned.

At great speed, Dharma broke into the clearing. "Enough!" he shouted, jumping between the demon and Tej, kukri in hand.

"Old man!" said the monster.

Dharma didn't hesitate and struck Mahisha's arm, lopping off some flesh. Mahisha's arm grew back almost immediately. On the ground, the chunk of flesh bubbled and took the form of a small two-legged fish-scaled creature with clawed hands. In the blink of an eye, Mahisha transformed into a mangy tiger with thorny skin. It bellowed a heinous unearthly sound. "You should know by now!" the demon spat. "Cutting me only makes me stronger!"

As the scaly creature mauled Tej with its vicious teeth, Dharma snatched it, mincing it with his kukri. "Leave us be! We want nothing from you."

Just beneath Mahisha's skin, the faint outline of human limbs and faces pushed against his membrane-like flesh. "This is all your fault!" growled the demon.

Arjuna jumped from terrace to terrace toward his older brother, his protector, but he was running out of time. A few more strides and he sprung at Mahisha, ready to slay the beast. But Mahisha hissed acid in his eyes, sending Arjuna reeling backward, clutching his face, blinded. The beast charged at him.

From the ground, Tej saw his brother being brutalized and rose back to his feet defiantly, his fists clenched.

Mahisha found this amusing. "Such mighty weapons you possess!"

As the *asura* moved in on Arjuna, Tej attacked using his fists, elbows, and knees.

Arjuna blindly swiped with his dagger, nearly slicing Tej, and it was Dharma who pulled him out of harm's way.

Mahisha swatted Arjuna like a fly then flung him into the high branch of a tree.

Devi fast approached the demon, armed with both kukris.

Dharma rushed at her, holding her back.

Mahisha once again overpowered Tej, chomping down on his hand, leaving only a shredded nub in its place. His cruelty didn't end there, and he pounded the defenseless young man over and over again. Tej felt a bone in his spine clunk out of place. Then another. And instantly, the feeling in his legs vanished. He made a futile grunt, as he lay beneath Mahisha, prostrate and gasping for breath, unable now to wriggle his remaining fingers.

He saw clearly that he had gravely underestimated the demon and that he should have acted with less haste, less bluster and bravado.

"Beast. From what hell have you been sent?"

"You can see it now!" Mahisha sang.

Devi pushed toward the demon, but Dharma shoved her back and held her in place. "No, Dharma! No! Why are you doing this!"

He did not answer.

Mahisha picked up Tej's limp frame in his jaws and backed toward the forest.

Arjuna madly wiped the acid from his eyes to clear his sight. Bleary-eyed, he climbed down the tree and rushed toward the demon carrying off his brother. As Tej opened his mouth to speak, blood spilled forth. "Stay, Arjuna," he insisted. "I've met my fate. Now you make yours."

Arjuna stopped in his tracks and watched his brother's eyes close for the last time, as the demon disappeared into the thick of the trees. He was stunned, his mind flooded with thoughts. He should have done more to save his brother—from himself. He hadn't needed Tej to be a god, and he regretted with all his soul that he hadn't told him that. *Tej had been good enough as he was. He just didn't know it.* The guilt of his silence would now be trapped in Arjuna's chest—like a prison—for the rest of his life.

In the near distance, Dharma released his grip on Devi and replaced his kukri in its scabbard. She looked to the old man for answers, but he swiftly turned away without a word.

# RECRUITED

Dharma marched up the long stone staircase leading back to the village. His footsteps fell heavy, weighted down by Tej's violent death and Mahisha's return to the lower valley. Devi stayed close behind but dared not say a word.

Arjuna stormed up from behind and pulled Dharma around to face him. "What was that, Dharma!"

The old man knew no words would soothe the youth's boiling rage, so instead he stared down at the offending hand clutching his sleeve.

As if seeing himself from the outside, grasping the esteemed elder's shirt, Arjuna immediately released his hand in shame.

"It was a trap," offered Dharma. "Mahisha wanted you to follow him."

Unable to sustain Dharma's gaze, Arjuna turned on Devi. "And you! You knew my brother was all talk. But you let him go, anyway!" He shoved Devi backward, the stairs falling away dangerously. She accepted the blow, her guilt hanging heavy. Seething, he grabbed her by the collar, his other hand reaching for his kukri.

The young girl, Pukuli, was skipping down the steps toward them, when she saw the commotion. She fled back toward the village, passing Lieutenant Colonel Young, as he entered the narrow alleys of the village with his entourage.

Behind the English, the Welsh contingent followed. Lieutenant Anwyl palmed his cherished books and stuck near to Captain Hughes, his protector.

This was not lost on Young. "It looks like Hughes has himself a new lap dog," he said to his compatriots.

"More like a Welsh terrier, sir," added Smith, who was combing his hair flat against his head like slick duck feathers.

Young expressed vague amusement then barked at the Welsh ranks, "Let's get a move on! I'm not going village to bloody village to sight-see! We need to raise a battalion in less than a week!"

"What happened to our leisurely hunting expedition?" Private Hardie asked his Welsh countrymen.

"O, perhaps our fearless leader with his *most excellent shot* hunted all the game to extinction," Private Cadogan mocked.

"He couldn't hit the side of a barn at three paces," chided Hardie.

Hughes hushed the banter, his tone serious. "Be sharp, boys. Orders have come to gather hillmen for our army."

"Not that I give a crap, but what for this time?" growled Private Maddocks.

"Ferdinand was assassinated," offered Hughes.

"Who's that?" another soldier asked.

"Archduke Franz Ferdinand," replied Anwyl. "Heir to the Austro-Hungarian throne."

"And what's that gotta do with us then?" Hardie pressed.

"Well, private, a Serb was the killer, and Austria-Hungary just declared war on Serbia, who they blame for trying to destroy the empire," said Hughes. "And based on the cable that arrived at headquarters in Pokhara and delivered to us this morning, I expect there's going to be war on the continent. A big one."

"How do you figure?" prodded Cadogan.

"They have us collecting a thousand soldiers for the front in this area alone," said Hughes, patiently. "And I imagine this is happening all over. You don't go to the edges of the empire to make an army—unless you are trying to amass a sizeable force."

When the soldiers arrived at the village centre, a small market was already underway with vegetables laid out on lengths of fabric. Several older men sat together deep in conversation. Arjuna's father poured alcohol into the wooden bowls before them.

"We have all seen that Mahisha's kingdom is getting bigger by the day," said the village elder, Mukhiya.

"I fear that if we don't deal with him now, it will soon be too late, his powers matching those of the greatest gods," said the youngest of the elders, whose face and arms were disfigured with pockmarks.

"But we know better than anyone," said Mukhiya. "Mahisha can't be defeated by mortals. For every death we avenge—he strikes back with three times the fury."

"Yes, perhaps Mahisha is best left alone," said Arjuna's father. "It's even possible we can live together in peace."

"And Mahisha doesn't pay us for our troubles like the British," added Mukhiya, jangling coins in a small pouch.

An elder in white robes quietly listened to the exchange and opened his mouth to speak. But instead of saying anything, he sighed in resignation.

In unison, they poured the first drops of alcohol to the ground as a libation. They all drank and made sour faces. "In all the Himalayas, no one makes rice wine like my wife does!" said Mukhiya.

They rumbled in agreement.

Pukuli burst into the square, arms flailing. "Arjuna's trying to kill Dev!"

The villagers fell silent. Arjuna's father regarded the situation gravely, but he looked relieved when he saw Devi stride into the square with Arjuna right behind. Clearly, things had not yet gotten to the boiling point.

Mukhiya eyed Devi. "I don't trust the stranger."

Devi faced Arjuna, bowed, and offered him Tej's kukri. Arjuna stared at the knife long and hard. "What have you done?" He snatched back his brother's knife.

Arjuna lunged at her, but Devi jumped back.

They tumbled across the square, wrestling and kicking up dust, as Arjuna tried to tackle Devi to the ground. But each time he tried to pull her off balance, she managed to find her centre, standing firm but flexible like a tree in a tempest. Villagers gathered in a circle around Devi and Arjuna, chanting for Arjuna.

Dharma marched up to the other elders. "Stop this. Before someone gets hurt. Or worse."

"Let's give it a moment," said Mukhiya.

Facing Arjuna's kukri, she drew her own, which felt heavy in hand given the deadly circumstances.

"You brought Mahisha back to the valley. It's YOU he wants," Arjuna shouted at Devi, accusingly.

"Arjuna, I don't want this."

Arjuna slashed at her, but she moved like water beneath his knife. He stumbled but attacked again, hoping to catch the stranger off balance. She effortlessly flowed around him.

"Are you going to fight?" spat Arjuna. "Or run away like a girl?"

"A warrior should choose his words more carefully than his battles," she warned.

Arjuna swung his blade at Devi. She spun, and their knives met with a metallic clang. Arjuna shoved her across the plaza.

Devi defied gravity, floating through the air, and managed to land on her feet.

Those gathered couldn't help but be impressed with the stranger's fighting prowess. But they also recognized that in the short time the outsider had been among them, he had somehow already upset the calm of the village.

Arjuna jumped at her but met Devi's leg, knocking him off balance. He was sweating, huffing, and working hard to counter her every move. He pinned her foot with his heel. She moved close, so close they could feel each other's breath on their cheeks. For Arjuna, the intimacy was intolerable. He shoved her back then thrust his kukri, but she sidestepped the weapon and countered with a palm strike to the elbow.

The knife flew from his grasp.

In a blur of motion, Arjuna kicked, but Devi jumped his leg. He swung back, striking her stomach. The crowd groaned in sympathy, as Devi rolled toward the plaza wall with the image of Devi Goddess. She looked up. Arjuna snatched up his dagger and closed in. Devi scuttled back, meeting the wall.

"You've got nowhere to go," said Arjuna, threatening. "Leave the village. You've done enough harm already."

Like a spider, Devi climbed backward up the wall and floated over Arjuna's head. He spun to face her. Devi flashed her empty right hand.

Arjuna looked on, uncomprehending.

She looked to Dharma, who nodded for her to proceed.

With her left hand, she swiped with the knife, leaving a long cut across his cheek. "I'm sorry," she whispered.

Arjuna touched his bloody cheek. "Why do you keep trying to humiliate me?"

"Enough," said Arjuna's father from the edge of the crowd. Arjuna clamoured to fight on but his father shouted again, and this time Arjuna untangled himself from Devi.

Across the plaza the British contingent stood watching, uncertain how to proceed. "Is this how the Gurkhas resolve their conflicts?" whispered Cadogan.

"If it is, we'll win the war in Europe in no time," said Hardie.

Devi offered Arjuna a hand up, but he ignored her.

To his father, Arjuna said, "Tej is dead."

"What?"

"Killed by the demon."

Dharma wordlessly affirmed the truth.

Arjuna's father bowed his head in grief, burdened by his recent words dismissing Mahisha's threat, wondering now if his inaction had cost his son's life.

"Dharma, we need to go back right now," said Devi. "And slay Mahisha!"

"There has been enough blood for one day."

With that, Dharma walked away.

\*

Hours later, the village market began anew, though it remained sub-dued after the news of Tej's tragic death. The British contingent moved into the square and placed a small wooden box on the ground at the feet of Lieutenant Colonel Young. He stepped up on it and addressed the villagers, speaking with great self-importance to ensure he made an impression upon his audience: "In Britain's hour of need, our most faithful allies—the Gurkhas—have fought alongside us."

"Who has time to fight?" shouted a villager. "We're farmers."

"These British come only to harvest our best young men, leaving us with nothing," said an older lady. "When I was a child, my father died fighting for them in the Second Anglo-Afghan War."

"And let's not forget, they bring their diseases," said the elder with the pock scars on his arms and face.

But a tension soon bubbled to the surface between several village youth and the elders. A young man spoke up, "But it was uncle's wage from serving with the British that paid for his big plot of land. Now he lives like a king! Why should we not have such opportunities?"

"Believe me, the price was too high," said the woman, who had lost her father.

The lieutenant colonel did his best to ignore the peasants' chatter. "This battle will be swift, and the Germans will put up little resistance when faced with our vast superiority. And, in the meantime, you will earn a good wage, see the civilized world, and be home for Christmas—"

"*Ehm*, tell them they'll be home by the next planting season," Hughes politely corrected his commander. "They don't celebrate Christmas."

Young ignored his advice. Still, the villagers appeared restless, and this secretly concerned him. Then he remembered a name he had heard several times in the villages. *Mahisha*. A demon. An *asura*. He appealed to the villagers: "With the help of fierce warriors like you, we can slay Britain's Mahisha, our *asura*."

Arjuna crossed the plaza toward the crowd gathered around the British, with Devi following at a safe distance.

"What's he saying?" Arjuna asked of the crowd, his eyes still glossy with tears.

"Something about fighting demons," said a middle-aged farmer, leaning on his shovel like a crutch.

This meant something to Devi. "So you are now prepared to fight the demon?"

"Why, yes!" exclaimed Young, pleased by the positive reaction from the crowd.

"And we will be stronger together!"

A young woman, Uruwasi, silently admired Arjuna, as he scowled in Devi's direction.

Hovering near Devi was the girl, Pukuli, who declared to the village, "I want to be a Gurkha, too!"

"Ha! No girls allowed!" said Badri, the rail thin villager. "Only the bravest of the brave!"

"The warrior I am is because of my mother," Devi snapped at Badri, before casting an approving look at Pukuli, who reciprocated with a smile.

Arjuna stepped toward the lieutenant colonel. "For this noble cause, I'll fight."

Young pulled on his moustache, approvingly.

Devi stepped forward to join Arjuna, but he immediately took a step away from her, as if she was contagious. His scorn was not lost on her, but the awkward moment was quickly buried by the flood of volunteers that gathered around the British.

"Once and for all, we'll defeat Mahisha!" shouted Devi.

Young chose not to correct her and instead announced, "So we've got ourselves an army! And let's hope you live up to your reputation!"

Pukuli's father raised his kukri in the air. "Ayo Gurkhali!"

Other village men thrust their fists and knives in the air and cried out in unison, "Ayo Gurkhali!"

*

It took several weeks for the mobilized men of Dharma's village to receive their marching orders. During that time, Tej's body could not be cremated, nor could his ashes be scattered. After all, Mahisha had stolen away the body where it couldn't be found. The priests of the village led the three-day ceremony in an attempt to cremate the soul, which would aid in its journey to the land of the dead. The men and women of Tej's family—from the village as well as outlying communities—took part. There was much dancing and feasting, as well as hopeful offerings of food and clothing to appease the uneasy soul and assist with its transmigration. No one wanted a restless soul wandering amongst them, as it could bring grave misfortune.

Finally, an effigy of Tej was taken to the top of the ridge above the village, where the priests prepared it for release, praying and advising the soul of its choice to either reincarnate or dwell in the land of ancestors. But there was a disruption, and a secret divination ceremony revealed to the priests that the soul had not journeyed onward, perhaps because of the nature of Tej's unnatural death by the demon. For the sake of the village, the priests kept that truth to themselves and prepared a secret ritual to assist in the release of the burdened soul.

With the belief that Tej's soul had successfully moved onward, village life began to return to normal. And now in the plaza, with army uniforms being distributed by the British, festive music played on a damphu drum and a high-pitched woodwind instrument, while hundreds of villagers milled about, drinking from wooden cups. There was much merry-making, and many of the men wore necklaces of lotus petals, including the two youngest recruits, Arjuna and Devi.

But Arjuna had remained hostile toward Devi since his brother's death and their public fight in the plaza, so she kept a safe distance. Still, she would find reasons to pass his home on the lower terraces in the hopes of glimpsing him.

An elephant adorned with paints and bangles kneeled on the ground, while a Tibetan mastiff weaved its way through the square, herding a flock of sheep toward the hills.

A line of village men waited their turn to pick up their military kit from a make-shift table manned by Captain Hughes. Lieutenant Colonel Young stood to the side, not wishing to fraternize with the new recruits. He turned to Smith and said, "Well, the Royal Rana of Gorkha has been paid handsomely for his assistance raising the battalion. Now he can finally pack up his entourage and head home. And we can be spared his ghastly banquets and useless banter."

"Here-here," said Smith, dutifully.

Rakesh looked at Badri, an oversized military uniform hanging from his gaunt frame. "Turn him side-ways, and his enemies will never see him coming! Lie him flat, and his enemies will have a door mat!"

Badri pointed to Devi. "At least, I'm more man than he'll ever be with that long hair."

"We'll soon see about that," said Pukuli's father.

When Devi arrived at the front of the line, she stood facing Captain Hughes, who Devi had first encountered back in her own village months before. He looked at her puzzled. "Haven't we met?"

"No," she said, quickly.

"Well, then. Sign here," he said. He dipped her thumb in ink and pressed it into a logbook. Devi received a uniform.

"Why do we need these to fight the demon?" she asked.

"Only fools believe in demons!" the lieutenant colonel said with contempt.

"Just because *you* can't see them, doesn't mean they aren't real," Devi retorted, her eyes fixed on Young. Then, in a flash, it occurred to her. "You tricked us. With all your talk of slaying demons."

Young shrugged. The accusation meant nothing to him.

Badri slapped his knee and forced a grating laugh. "Ha! Dev thought we were going to war with Mahisha!"

"Hush, you stupid doormat," said Pukuli's father. "We all did!"

Arjuna, who stood behind Devi awaiting his uniform, flushed red but remained motionless in his place.

"Young man," said Hughes, kindly, to Devi. "You must have misunderstood. There's a war in Europe. With Germany."

Devi's mouth went dry with the revelation, and she turned back to Young, angry. "You can't make us go."

He, in turn, raised the logbook with Devi's fingerprint. "You see this? It's a contract. You belong to us now. Or would you rather the stockades?"

"I'd rather prison than fight for you."

"You'll enjoy spending the best years of your life in a cramped cell," he said, doing his best to stare Devi down. But her steadfast gaze unnerved him. "Well, then, is that what you want?"

"And throw away the key, while you're at it!"

Young spat at Devi's feet and signaled for two British soldiers to take the troublesome villager away. "Give him twenty lashes!"

"Make it forty!" she called back.

Arjuna's father watched this exchange with great concern.

As Devi was dragged away, Arjuna coughed to get the lieutenant colonel's attention. "I admit that I, too, misunderstood what we were fighting. I am, as you can see, a simple farmer now dressed in a soldier's uniform. Still, I am reporting for duty...sir."

Devi looked back. "Arjuna! What're you doing?"

"My brother would want me to go. To make our people proud. Besides, Mahisha isn't going anywhere. When I get back, I'll be ready for him."

"But we're ready now!"

"No," said Arjuna. "We aren't."

Just then, Arjuna's father sped across the plaza toward Devi, as she was being hauled away by the soldiers. He pushed in close and whispered, "If you go, we will gather the villagers to fight Mahisha in your absence. You have my word."

"Move back, old man!" said a soldier.

Arjuna's father stopped in his tracks but held his gaze on Devi.

She eyed Mahisha's mountain kingdom in the distance then dragged her heels in the dirt, halting the soldiers in their tracks.

"Wait," she called out.

Lieutenant Colonel Young lifted his eyes to meet hers. He smiled, amused. "So you've finally seen the light?"

"I will fight your war."

"Good!" Young tapped his pistol strapped to his waist. "Disobey my orders again, and it shall not be lashes you receive."

# ENTERING THE BEAST

The sound of music and festivities from the village faded into the rushing sound of water, as Devi kneeled before the bank of the river. With her kukri, she sliced off chunks of her long hair, which floated away downstream. After a time, her hair was cropped close to the scalp, with some tufts that missed the knife standing out like blades of untamed grass.

Then she took a deep breath and felt beneath her blouse. Her hand traced her body, exploring all her parts. She felt her arms and shoulders, which were powerful from a life of labour. A hand came to her chest. Her breasts had been growing in recent months, but she had dared not look, keeping them hidden beneath loose clothing. And now that she had committed herself to being male, and a soldier, it would require great care to maintain the charade. Not the least, hiding her menstrual blood. There would be no more banishment to the shed during her period to protect the family from bad luck, and she would not miss that.

But the consequences of being found out, she knew, would be grave. A surge of feelings threatened to overwhelm her. But she forced down her emotions, the ones that insisted she was a girl—almost a woman. The ones that wished to be near Arjuna. She hated the lie, but for now she had to live it.

Using a length of fabric, Devi tightly bound her chest, wrapping it around herself with slow intention. She had to work hard to breathe in a full lung of air with the fabric cinched like a noose around her frame. When she finished binding herself, she traced both hands down her flattened chest and felt a momentary thrill at the deception.

*

It was late in the evening, and the rain pattered on the pagoda roof of the village temple, which loomed in a veil of mist. Inside, the lamps burned, illuminating large wooden beams and elaborate carvings of Hindu gods. In a British military uniform, Devi bowed at the altar with the brass statue of the supreme goddess, Devi, adorned in red robes and draped with garlands of flowers and jewels. Offerings lay at her feet, including pieces of gold and silver, yellow mustard seeds, and plates of sheep meat sacrificed to please the goddess.

"...Let me rise on smoke and flame. Like a prayer to the heavens," she whispered, before placing down flowers at the altar.

As she prepared to stand, Arjuna's father emerged from the shadows by the doorway, soaking wet. His usual upright posture had sagged, burdened by the emotional weight of losing one son to the demon and soon another to a war in a faraway land. She stood to greet the elder, but he bowed first in deference, which she received with uncertainty.

"My son," he said sorrowfully. "He has physical strength—but you. You possess something more divine." Then he implored, "Please, protect him from harm."

She pressed her hands together and bowed.

After the unusual encounter with Arjuna's father, Devi made her way down the steps leading up to the temple, passing dozens of bells hanging from an old iron railing, which made the auspicious sound of *OM*, when rung.

The rain continued to fall, and small rivers formed in every depression in the earth. A rumble of thunder echoed through the valley followed closely by a bolt of lightning that struck the top point of the temple like a divine message of warning. Devi looked back then fled down the steps.

In the faint light of dawn, Dharma's village slumbered. A slow clanging bell tolled, echoing through the valley. The land surrounding Mahisha's mountain kingdom continued to burn and smoulder, while cracks in the earth appeared like lesions, boiling with molten fire.

Inside Dharma's hut, Devi and the old man sat sleeplessly by the fireplace. Her military rucksack rested on the ground by the door. They knew they might not see each other for a long time and neither wanted to leave the other's side.

"I have so many questions," she said, breaking the silence.

"Speak, young man."

"Why do you say so little?"

"Perhaps ask yourself why so many feel the need to fill space with empty words." He smiled to himself. "A single moment of silence contains the infinite. Have you ever experienced that feeling of the eternal when your mind grows absolutely still?"

A look of recognition crossed her face, and she nodded in the affirmative.

Satisfied, he gazed at her a long while. He had only met Dev a few short months ago, as she fought Mahisha's demon dogs while bravely trying to save her mother. Yet, strangely, he felt closer to the outsider than anyone else in the village.

"I know you know suffering," he finally said. "Grief is a heavy weight, particularly in the early days. And even as it lifts, it will always remain in the shadows. Yes, maybe in happier times," he continued, "the grief recedes with the shadows. But remain mindful that in darker times, those shadows move closer, and the grief can overwhelm you once again. This is all part of what it is to be human."

"And what about the gods? Do they feel such grief?"

"Young man," he grinned. "That I do not know." Then he regarded her seriously. "But make no mistake, there will be scars. In a time before you were born, smallpox swept through this village. We lost a third of our people. Imagine that. Mothers, sons, uncles, friends. All dead. So the outbreak is now in the past, yes, but many of us still suffer the consequences—losing a child, a father, being disfigured by the terrible disease, or gripped by fear that it could happen all over again."

Devi eyed the old wooden trunk sitting in the corner of the room with the words *British East India Co.* written on its side. She had seen it many times but had never paid it much mind.

"What's in the box?" she asked.

With a gesture, he invited her to look inside.

She opened the trunk and began to lift out exotic items the likes of which she had never seen. Each heirloom she held up to the candlelight: a silver flask with the words engraved: *Cpt Akasha*, a wooden flintlock pistol with an ornate trigger and hammer, a stale smelling wooden box imprinted with the words *Por Larrañaga, Habana, Cuba*. In view of the shaman's masks on the wall, Devi held up an elegant red velvet dress.

Dharma regarded the child with curiosity, as she gazed at the dress with great interest. The curving neckline trimmed in gold. The details along the sleeve.

Each item she uncovered hinted at a world beyond the village. And perhaps, she thought, it hinted at a life Dharma had once lived before this one. In time, she carefully placed the dress and all the items back in the trunk.

"You knew the British weren't sending us to fight Mahisha," she said. "And yet you said nothing."

"You could not see beyond your lust for revenge, and so you did not hear what the British were asking of you."

"Was this your way of getting rid of me?"

"No, young man. This is your home—now and always," he said.

Devi sighed heavily. "How do I take action when I'm so full of doubt?"

"You can't know what you don't know. Enter into every situation with acceptance and a sense of openness."

"But you didn't accept me when we first met."

He laughed, sadly. "I never said I was perfect. The truth is you can't force people to accept you or to change themselves. All you can do is be yourself and the rest is up to the universe."

She remained in her place, staring.

"I see you still have more questions."

"I don't get it," she finally said. "We were so close to getting Mahisha."

"I thought that once before. And I led many young men to their slaughter. After that, Mahisha, well, left us alone. And we left it at that."

"So when did he come back?"

Dharma hedged.

"It's me, isn't it? I'm bad luck. I know it."

"Perhaps in this other land where you're being sent you'll find more answers to your questions," Dharma offered.

Devi stared at the wall, troubled. The hollow eyes of a wooden shaman's mask with long hair stared back, its mouth down-turned in a frightful manner.

"It wasn't supposed to be like this."

Dharma poked the fire in the hearth with a stick, his eyes half-closed in a weary-sadness.

"What is he?" Devi asked. "I deserve to know. He destroyed everything I loved."

"Mahisha? I'm afraid he's a ghostly shadow of himself."

"Was he once human?"

"Actually, he was just like you."

"He's nothing like me!"

"You're both orphans," said Dharma, patiently. "One day, a deceitful god transformed his pain into something monstrous."

Devi sat beside Dharma, staring at the old man and the revelations he was suddenly spilling forth. "Dharma. I don't understand."

"We're all demons and gods. All of us. Without love, even the power of the greatest god is blind." Dharma placed Devi's hand on his heart. "True power lies here...where no masks can be worn." Behind him, the shamanic masks stared down, silently bearing witness.

Dharma untied the sheathed kukri from his belt and drew the knife. "The same fire that gave birth to our people also forged this magical kukri."

"Magical?" she stumbled, stunned by his words. "But how did you come to possess such a divine weapon?"

The old man looked down at his hands and did not answer. Then he whispered, "Some stories are meant to remain in the realm of myth."

With that, he replaced the kukri in its sheath and presented it to her, but she refused outright. Unwavering, he held out the sacred knife.

"I'm not worthy," she pleaded.

"I hope one day you realize you are."

Finally, Devi bowed and accepted. She untied her old, rusted knife and offered it to Dharma. "It belonged to my father's father."

Dharma wiped the dirt from the blade. An inscription on it read: *TO MY CHILD. FORGED WITH THE LOVE OF A FATHER.*

"A true gift of love," he said. He held the knife back out to her. After all, it was a gift too important to give away. Her gentle hand pressed it back toward him, and he accepted the family heirloom with a deep bow of gratitude.

*

The sun had not yet climbed above the jagged ridge of mountains, while the snow blowing from the summits looked like mysterious veils in the blue light. From the villages dotting the valley, large numbers of men filed out on foot and horseback along the dirt paths. Rising up along the dirt track, the Gurkha soldiers sang, "...It's better to die...than be a coward..."

Lieutenant Colonel Young proudly rode his horse alongside the newly raised battalion. Among the faces marching by was Arjuna, who eyed Devi warily. Devi stopped and turned to look back at the village. Mahisha's kingdom rose above on the blackened slopes, while fissures in the earth revealed a bubbling molten world beneath. Hughes and Anwyl followed her gaze but saw only snow-covered summits with green slopes beneath.

From behind, Devi felt a push, as Pukuli's father gently directed Devi onward.

Badri, with the pencil moustache, said to the others, "I heard Germans are twelve feet tall with massive hands that can crush a human!"

Rakesh brandished his kukri. "They may be big, but our knives are sharper."

The soldiers' laughter rose into the hills and carried all the way to Bombay Harbour, where there was much activity surrounding the docked transport ship. There, thousands of Gurkhas and Indian soldiers, weighted down with military kit, walked up the gangplanks onto the ship. Up above, cranes lifted horses and cannons into the cargo hold. Troops leaned against the railings, smoking and waving good-bye to loved ones below.

At the foot of a gangplank, Devi stood in awe. She had never been in a city or seen an endless body of water like the one outstretched beyond the wharf. Nor had she ever seen a ship, and she was absolutely confounded how something so large could stay afloat. She needed time to process all the wonders she was witnessing. And it occurred to her that Dharma had most likely been here before, that he was familiar with the flat lands and all the buildings and crowds and even the choppy ocean. A glimpse of his past had been revealed in his East India trunk back in the village.

Nearby, Arjuna wordlessly studied the outsider. The future had not yet revealed itself, and he was deeply worried. Strangely, though, he felt more hopeful knowing Dev would be with him for the journey.

Just as the sun set, the ship pulled away from the long jetty and steamed toward the infinite—where water met sky in a perfect blend of reds, oranges, and yellows.

*

The haunting sound of bagpipes and the pounding of artillery seemed an unfathomable distance from the open sea, but within weeks of leaving Bombay, Devi and her compatriots had disembarked at the Port of Boulogne-sur-Mer, France, ridden a train to Poperinghe in Belgium, been hastily instructed in the ways of combat, then marched another seven miles along muddy roads to a stone outpost several miles from the front.

A dark rain fell from the sky, as Captain Hughes and his men gathered. Devi watched as hundreds of black men in uniform chopped down trees, dug latrines, and unloaded countless artillery shells from the rail flatbeds—all under the critical gaze of British officers.

Hughes saw Devi's discontent. "Black people from the empire aren't allowed on the front lines," he said, regretfully.

"The British empire was not built on equality," declared Anwyl.

"Especially in the Caribbean," Hughes added.

"What's a Caribbean?" asked Rakesh, puzzled.

"Have you never seen a map of the world, private?"

All the Gurkhas shook their heads.

"I will show you the world. When I get my hands on a map."

The soldiers of Devi's company fell silent, standing rigid, as they gazed across the sweeping horizon toward the jagged remains of the gothic town Ypres illuminated by the flash of artillery.

When they were given the order to take up positions on the frontlines, they pushed forward through the deep mud. Artillery exploded on either side, showering them with debris. And the closer to the front they got, the more ghastly the landscape, with bloated bodies and dead horses floating in the rain-filled craters.

Alongside Devi, Captain Hughes kept pace, while Arjuna, Rakesh, and Private Maddocks remained close. Lieutenant Anwyl, who always stayed close to Hughes' side, wore a mask of terror and tried desperately to keep up. Badri was falling dangerously behind and hollered to the others to slow down.

A German biplane sputtered overhead.

"A flying demon!" cried Badri.

They passed a large number of bodies with faces twisted in agony, if they had heads at all. Many wore Canadian uniforms, as well as British, French, Indian, and Australian uniforms. Devi saw Arjuna abruptly split off from the group.

"Where are you going?" she shouted, but he couldn't hear her above the chaos of war. Devi went in pursuit.

Arjuna dug his heels into the earth trying to free something from the mud. Pukuli's father was chest deep in muck, his packsack dragging him down. As Arjuna pulled at his arm, his feet sunk deeper and deeper into the sticky mud.

Devi came up from behind, palmed Arjuna's backpack, and tugged like mad, bracing herself against a fallen tree underfoot. Explosions rattled the earth, the ground shuddering like violent earthquakes.

Arjuna looked back at Devi, stony-eyed and determined.

The pack on Pukuli's father continued to weigh him down.

"Get it off!" she shouted.

"I won't survive a day out here without it!" he shouted back.

"With it, you won't survive another minute! If you want to see your daughter again, take the pack off right now!"

He released his grip and slipped off the backpack. As he did, he sunk deeper into the slick clay. Arjuna snatched his hand and pulled hard. Immediately, Devi redoubled her efforts, hauling back on Arjuna's pack. There was a collective groan, as they used all their energy to free the trapped man. And slowly, Pukuli's father began to emerge from the mud like some sort of swamp monster.

"Let him go!" shouted Captain Hughes, the other Gurkhas huddled close behind. "You can't risk everyone—for a single comrade!"

"A true friend is worth a thousand risks!" Arjuna hollered back.

Devi redoubled her efforts, and Pukuli's father suddenly broke free from the soupy clutches of the earth. He rolled onto his back, relieved.

"Thank you," he said, grimly.

"Let's go!" shouted Hughes, and they all set off running once again.

Another hundred yards, and they had arrived at the front lines, their muddy boots landing in the bottom of the trench.

Badri landed in the mud but, overloaded with his military pack, lost his balance and tipped over.

"The weight of the empire is great," said Rakesh, offering Badri a hand up.

Captain Hughes approached Devi and Arjuna. "NEVER do that again," he commanded. "That's an order."

From a sandbag bunker emerged Lieutenant Colonel Young. Devi's face betrayed her contempt. "Long nose is here!?"

"You belong to his battalion," said Hughes. "Try not to forget that, private." Then he added: "What you did back there was incredibly brave. Stupid but brave." He rested a hand on Arjuna's shoulder. "Gentlemen, rest while you can. We'll be off soon enough."

"Where?" asked Arjuna.

"To visit the Germans, of course." Captain Hughes adjusted his glasses and departed down the trench. Filthy exhausted men slept, while the wounded lay in the mud, moaning. Rats scurried through the trench, feeding on the dead. A tired Australian smoked. A Canadian soldier read a letter.

Badri plugged his nose and retched. "What's that smell?"

Behind him, hands and feet dangled from the bodies entombed in the muddy trench wall.

*

It was early evening, when Arjuna and Devi dared to peer above the lip of the trench. Thousands of bodies, horses, and broken armour littered the pock-marked landscape. In the distance, an artillery shell struck a German position, sending flame and debris everywhere. For an instant, the shadow of a demon appeared in the pluming fireball.

Arjuna absorbed the sorrow of the battlefield, as if every lifeless body was that of his dead brother, Tej. He looked to Devi then sunk back to the bottom of the trench. With his red and yellow kerchief, Arjuna wiped his brow then tied it back around his neck. Soon they opened their tins of food and fed on the cold muck without enthusiasm.

As they ate, the artillery began to land in an almost continuous boom! Boom! Boom! Dust and debris showered hundreds of Gurkhas. Several soldiers could be heard weeping. Badri looked haunted. "We can't win against the machines."

Arjuna put down his can of food and bowed his head in prayer. "Oh, Lord Krishna and mother goddess, Devi. Protect us and help chase our enemies into the fire."

"Amen to that," said Hughes, who was huddled among the Welsh and Nepalese troops. "Gentlemen," he spoke up, after a long pause. "In a situation such as this, one can only set goals, not expectations of outcome. Our enemy is fierce, and I can't promise what will happen in this trench, let alone when we go over the top. So be ready. And Godspeed, one and all." He could think of nothing else to say, so he saluted and took his leave.

The night grew calm, as the opposing artillerymen took a break from terrorizing the battlelines. Some of the Gurkhas fell asleep, while others remained wide-eyed in terror. Arjuna shivered against the cold. Beside him, Devi looked up at the sky. She was surprised to see a phantom chariot ridden by the blue god, Krishna, race across the sky and vanish into the clouds. "Of course, you are here," she whispered, comprehendingly, to herself. "You are everywhere."

"What was that?" asked Arjuna, sleepily.

But then Devi perceived danger, the sound of approaching boot steps, faintly but rapidly growing louder. She held her breath as she listened, her senses alight. She tapped Arjuna's shoulder to alert him.

She unsheathed Dharma's magical kukri, just as the first Germans poured into the trench. "Ayo Gurkhali!" she shouted, raising the alarm across the trench.

The other Gurkhas unsheathed their kukris and shouted, "Ayo Gurkhali!"

A German soldier armed with a rifle and wearing a spiked helmet charged at her. A wash of smoke obscured everything. She charged forward into the smoke, kukri gripped tightly in hand, striking at everything in her path. As the smoke blew over, the German slumped lifelessly on the ground behind her.

Devi looked back with regret but was met by Rakesh's shouts: "Don't look back! There's more coming!"

And he was right. More Germans leapt down into the trench like a dam with a catastrophic breach.

Lieutenant Anwyl cowered from battle, flinching when a sharp whistle blew. Lieutenant Colonel Young appeared from the officer's bunker built into the trench, removing the whistle from his mouth. He stormed toward Anwyl. "I want every squarehead dead!" he shouted, resting a hand on his pistol. "And if any Mick, Taff, or Jock hasn't the courage to fight, I shall personally shoot him myself."

Captain Hughes swooped down on Anwyl, pulling him away as his superior officer was upon him. "He doesn't mean that," Hughes whispered to allay Anwyl's anxious look.

Devi closed the distance with another German soldier, diving under his weapon. An upward strike brought him down. In a continuous circular flow of motion, the glistening curved kukri encompassed then consumed enemy after enemy, taking out each one differently—head strike. Thigh strike. Throat strike.

Face to face with a burly German soldier, Arjuna put on an awesome display of knife work, swishing his kukri in sweeping motions around the soldier—without touching him. The German remained motionless like a stone statue. Only the slightest moan indicated he was still alive.

"Kill 'im, bloody hell!" shouted Corporal Smith from behind.

Arjuna paused his display of knife work. "How can I kill a man standing in the flesh who hasn't lifted a finger at me?"

The man still stood there in uniform, unable or unprepared to fight. "I'm a pacifist," the German said in broken English. "I...I refuse to fight my fellow man."

Arjuna looked back to see a glimmer of doubt on Smith's face. But the corporal's words said otherwise, "Tomorrow he could be the one tryin' to kill us!" Arjuna gripped his knife and stepped toward the German. But instead of bludgeoning the man, he kicked him hard in the ass and sent the soldier fleeing out of the trench.

"You tell them who we are!" Arjuna shouted after him. "*WE'RE GURKHAS!*"

Other Gurkhas and Welsh scrambled to fight off the Germans, firing their rifles and locked in hand-to-hand combat. Maddocks fired and shot his first German then looked to Cadogan, who nodded in grim approval.

A giant of a man confronted Devi, with a toothless grin. In an earlier time, maybe he had been a baker or a butcher or a farmer like her. But now he was a soldier, and he meant business. He swung his bayonet, slashing her shoulder. The giant's bayonet got trapped in the mud, so Devi aimed for his head with her kukri. His powerful forearm swung into her arm, so she redirected the strike to his knee, which buckled.

A short distance away, Arjuna battled a soldier armed with a lethal *Nahkampfmesser* combat knife.

As the giant man freed his bayonet, Devi ran up the edge of the bayonet and planted her feet on his shoulders. Her legs clamped tight on either side of his head, and she whirled like a fan, twisting the man's neck until it snapped. At once, his bones seemed to fail him, as if turned to dust, and he collapsed in a lifeless heap.

For a whiff of time, their eyes met. Devi paused, and all went silent. The giant's expression was sorrowful. Then the sound of other Gurkhas fighting around her returned—battle cries, clanging metal, gunfire, and artillery. A growl stole her attention, and she spun to face another German. Behind him, Arjuna and his opponent continued to fight to the death.

Devi stepped clear of the knife and cut him down with a slashing strike, as if chopping wood at home. But these were lives she was cutting short, and she knew that.

Pukuli's father moved up alongside Rakesh, a gleam in his eye. He looked to Devi. "He's small. But strong as a yak!"

Two German soldiers appeared before them, brandishing swords.

Pukuli's father dispatched one German, while Rakesh fought a fierce battle—sword against knife. He slipped in close and plunged the knife in.

Devi cleared away her latest victim and moved toward Arjuna, where a German soldier lorded over him, a knife pointed at his eye.

In the distance, Pukuli's father and Rakesh caught sight of Arjuna in trouble. As they raced toward him, Devi soared through the air, landing beside Arjuna's adversary.

She flashed her empty right hand. He looked to it, confused. Then she struck him in the throat with the kukri gripped in her left hand.

Behind her, the enemy began to flee. The Gurkhas roared with approval. "Ayo Gurkhali!"

"I can handle myself," Arjuna growled at Devi.

"A warrior's first duty is to protect. Besides, I promised your father I'd look out for you."

Arjuna wanted to stay mad at Dev for all that had happened back at his village, but the stranger's kindness wasn't making it easy for him to stay angry. Wordlessly, he turned away.

# OF GODS & WAR

The battlefield was quiet but for the occasional artillery shell that landed on either side of the front lines. The men in the muddy trenches wore their shattered nerves on their haggard faces, some recoiling with each exploding artillery round. Others, hardened by months of fighting, barely flinched, as they wandered the trenches in search of food, a cigarette, or a drip of alcohol. Without hesitation, some European soldiers stole from the dead. But the Nepalese remained deeply superstitious, fearing the wrath of the spirit-world, so they left the dead's possessions where they lay.

Lieutenant Anwyl approached the officer's bunker, his eyelids twitching from sleeplessness and fear. From the sandbag lair built into the trench and reinforced with old wooden beams, Captain Hughes emerged to greet him.

"You wanted to see me, sir?" said Anwyl, saluting.

"Yes, lieutenant. How are you fairing?"

"Sir, I've had better days. And, truthfully, never worse. Apologies for my frankness, but it's a living hell out here."

"In that case, what I have for you may not be to your liking..."

"Sir?" said Anwyl, inquiringly.

"Back in Nepal you lent me some magnificent books. And for that I'm grateful." With some hesitation, Hughes held out a book for the junior officer.

Anwyl gazed upon the book as if it were a bar of gold. It was *Heart of Darkness* by Joseph Conrad. "It's for me, captain?" he asked, eyes wide.

"Only if you fancy it." Hughes placed the book in his hand. "It's not the lightest subject, I recognize."

"Thank you, sir. I will cherish it."

"It's a book that will make any man, no matter how common, reflect on his inner nature."

"The way I see it, sir, all great art must jolt us from our everyday thinking." Anwyl grew more excited and, for a moment, forgot he dwelled in a deathly trench. "For me, I like to think about the world the artist lived in and the ideas of the time that shaped him."

"Indeed," said Hughes.

"After all, none of us are solitary trees in the desert, evolving alone."

Hughes smiled. "Lieutenant, you are clearly an ideas man."

"Like you, sir."

Concern coloured the captain's expression. He had known many soldiers in the field and the ones best suited for combat, he had come to learn, were those who grew up in the countryside, familiar with discomfort, guns, and even the act of killing—albeit animals, not fellow humans. Anwyl, he knew, was from a large town in Wales and had never held a gun before joining the military. It defied logic, but Hughes felt deeply afraid for Anwyl, as if he were his own kin.

Finally, Hughes said more soberly, "Ideas, yes, lieutenant. But out here, we also need courage and quick reflexes, because war is not easy."

"*Ie*, sir."

Hughes hedged. "I'm trying to impart to you that it's OK to be afraid. We're all afraid. It's also okay to be hopeful, as long as you prepare for the worst." Hughes looked around the trench filled with the living and dead. "Especially in a place like this."

"With all due respect, if you're asking me to be a realist, sir, I can assure you I am. I'm quite certain I'm going to die in this trench."

Hughes was at a loss for words then smiled sadly and said, "Well, off you go."

"As you wish, sir." Anwyl saluted and was on his way.

Further down the trench, Arjuna and Devi sat against the wall, shivering, their breath leaving vapor trails like dragons' breath. He raised a flask to the heavens then to Devi. He tipped a few drops of alcohol to the earth, took a drink, and passed along the flask.

"And to think I mistook you for a girl."

73

"Women can be just as fierce as any man."

Arjuna paused on her words before offering a thoughtful nod. "Still, you are as fierce as anyone I have ever known."

Devi took the compliment but bowed her head, as if unable to shoulder the weight of it. "My mother used to say I was special," she said, without bitterness. "But don't all parents think that?"

"Maybe it doesn't matter what we think, because life will find us, anyway," he said, eyeing their grim reality. Then he asked, "Sometimes you disappear at night. I always wonder where you go."

"To be alone for a minute or two, that's all." She didn't speak of her nightly escape behind the lines to relieve herself away from the eyes of men. Nor did she mention the field dressing kits she collected that included safety pins and the sterile gauze pads she stuffed down her pants during her period. For months, she had been stashing the safety pins in her rucksack for a use not yet known to her.

A long silence fell between them, and neither rushed to fill the emptiness.

With each swig of alcohol, Arjuna's thoughts grew more fractured, with flashes of the grisly war stitched together with fragments of home. His parents. The mountains. His dead brother when he was alive. None of it made sense.

Devi saw in Arjuna's slackened expression that he was temporarily lost.

"What are you thinking, Arjuna?"

"Just memories," he sighed. "Sometimes they feel more like a dream."

Devi touched his arm and passed back the flask.

Then he said what he had held inside for most of his life. "I was six when my mother died."

Devi nodded for him to continue. He didn't want to, but something within needed to escape, as if he had been holding his breath all these years.

"I didn't know what to do after she was gone. So I walked. Away from the village. And for a long time I wandered the forest. Out there, surrounded by wilderness, I didn't have any fear. It took me years to realize, but that day taught me that I belonged to no one. And no one belonged to me. Not even my parents. Then I was greeted by something." He stopped in thought, remembering the beautiful lake surrounded by green hills glowing in the late afternoon light.

"What did you see?"

"Hundreds of white lotus flowers floating. They were perfect. Rising from the muddy waters—but untouched by the dirt."

Arjuna remembered picking up a closed flower to admire. At once, the lotus opened, revealing another lotus inside it. That lotus opened and inside another lotus bloomed. Arjuna, the boy, looked down at his reflection and saw something move behind him.

"But when I saw her...I knew I belonged to one thing and one thing only..."

Arjuna's eyes fixed on Devi.

"Who did you see?" she asked.

"The great goddess, Devi."

She smiled, gently. "But you still have room for prayers to Lord Krishna, too."

"Of course," he grinned. "He loves devotion as much as cow's milk!"

Arjuna and Devi breathed close to one another, so close it was almost a kiss. The serene beauty of this young man, Dev, was too much for Arjuna, and it tore at him. *But what was wrong with admiring this near stranger?* Arjuna reasoned with himself. *Did I not admire my own father?* But he knew the feeling was much more than that. He quickly looked away and took a nervous tip from the flask.

That night, the men of the Gurkha battalion shivered and coughed in the cold damp, their bodies remaining close to one another to conserve body heat.

Devi curled up facing Arjuna, his red and yellow kerchief around his neck. Asleep, Arjuna took hold of her hand. Devi relaxed and drew closer.

For hours, they lay like that, and Devi felt an intimacy she had never experienced before. Then Arjuna awoke to find himself holding Devi's hand and yanked himself free from her grasp. Devi pulled back, stung by the rejection. But she understood such painful feelings were foolish. After all, she was the one pretending to be a man. And what did she risk by revealing her secret to Arjuna? *Rejection? Even death?* She turned away, slipping his kerchief inside her shirt.

*

For months, the disfigured battle lines remained firmly in place, etched into the muddy terrain of Belgium—despite the artillery barrages and the continuous back and forth orders to attack the opposing trenches across miles of deadened land. Only when a temporary calm was restored would brave men scurry out to no-man's-land with stretchers to recover the shattered bodies amid the debris.

During one such lull in the fighting, Field Marshal John French, commander of the Western Front, made the dangerous journey to the front lines and arrived in the officers' bunker to brief his junior staff. The officers stood at attention and saluted the field marshal when he made his entrance. After a long speech about the necessity of personal sacrifice, he stepped before Lieutenant Colonel Young and his well-oiled moustache.

"Congratulations lieutenant colonel," he said, gruffly. "They located your superior's body. His head, most unfortunately, wasn't found. You've just made colonel."

"I will prove I'm worthy," Young gushed.

"You should be more concerned with impressing your men. They're the ones dying for you."

Just outside the bunker, the Gurkhas squatted on their haunches, some cleaning their fingernails, oiling their rifles, or trying to rest. Rakesh sharpened his kukri and tested the sharpness with his finger. He dragged his kukri against a stone, creating sparks to start a small fire. Exploding mortars and gunfire punctuated their activities.

Overhead, black carrion crows circled the overcast skies. It had been cold and cloudy for weeks now, and morale had pitched downward.

Badri hugged his knees around his chest as he napped, trying to sleep off the nightmare of war, hoping to wake up back in his beloved village.

Rakesh pointed at Badri asleep against the trench wall. "At least if he dies in his sleep, they'll say he died doing what he did best."

Lieutenant Anwyl along with Maddocks were walking past the Gurkha contingent when Anwyl noticed Arjuna praying before the image of the goddess Devi. "Say," he asked the Nepalis. "Why do you have so many gods?"

Pukuli's father answered kindly: "We didn't choose to have so many gods. They chose us. They are all aspects of the Divine Brahman."

"We are a dankish fool-born lot," said Maddocks, dismissively. "We make our world, imagine our gods into existence. Heaven and hell are on earth, because we pignuts make it that way. This war," he added, "was made by men. Not feuding gods. Worse even, we have flap-mouthed louts shouting orders for us to kill ourselves wave after wave. That's the English way."

Arjuna tried to ignore them, as he prayed before the image of the goddess propped up in his makeshift altar in the trench wall.

"Well," said a Nepali soldier from another village. "I'm a Buddhist."

"You can be a Buddhist and still believe in the Hindu gods," said another. "At least where I come from."

Nearby, Hardie and several of his countrymen reinforced a section of trench that had collapsed after a recent attack by the Germans. "I don't get it," said Hardie, in a friendly manner. "How come your gods have so many hands and heads? It's hard to believe."

"You have to believe to see them," said Pukuli's dad.

"Hey Welshman," called out Rakesh. "You have God in your bible, no?"

"*Ie.*"

"So if you can believe in one god, why do you find it so hard to believe in a thousand gods?"

The Welshman shrugged.

"Well," continued Rakesh. "If you believe in an apple, why wouldn't you believe in the apple after someone has sliced it into hundreds of little pieces? That's not much of a stretch of the imagination is it now."

"I suppose not," said Hardie.

Devi kept to herself, silently cleaning the kukri given to her by Dharma. She had her doubts about its magical qualities but wanted to believe that it provided her with extra protection. She stole a glance of Arjuna bowed before the image of the supreme goddess, his handsome face strained with worry.

Pukuli's father sat beside Devi and opened a tin can with his knife. A Nepalese soldier watched Devi with an equal measure of awe and suspicion. "I've seen you killed a thousand times in battle, and yet you somehow always make it back. You're lucky to be alive."

"We all are," Arjuna responded, without turning away from his altar.

"That wasn't luck," Pukuli's father said. He pointed to his head. "Fate is written here."

Just down the way, Anwyl and Maddocks joined Hardie and Cadogan, whose bright blue eyes had been dulled by the war. As the Welsh continued to reinforce the trench walls, Hardie rested his tired sights on Devi. In a low voice, he whispered, "This is gonna sound absolutely bonkers."

"Go on, boy," prodded Cadogan.

"Well, for a man, Dev makes a pretty good-looking bird."

There were loud groans from the other men.

"Hardie," growled Maddocks. "This place already smells of death and arse. And now ya gotta say pig-brained crap like that? You shall not live that down any time soon, I promise you. It's bad enough we have a reputation for sheep."

"Which one is that?"

His words were met with amused snickers from the Welsh.

At the other end of the trench, a group of British drank from bottles and flasks and were staggering about merry-making.

"What do they have to celebrate?" sneered Arjuna.

"*You'll be home for Christmas,*" mocked Rakesh, imitating Young.

"They enthusiastically treat us like loyal dogs, not their equals," said Pukuli's father.

"I'd serve beside a Tibetan mastiff over them any day," Rakesh grumbled.

A Nepali soldier trying to fix his rifle threw it down in disgust. "And they always give us the worst equipment."

Rakesh raised his kukri. "That's why I only fight with this. It never jams and doesn't need reloading."

Another Gurkha soldier rattled his smashed compass, sullenly.

Devi regarded the discontent, peered above the lip of the trench, then bolted. The others watched after her with concern.

Several blistering rounds of artillery landed in no-man's-land, blowing out a wash of debris and metal fragments. Where once stood entire forests, now only a matchstick of wood here and there rose from the earth. Devi picked through the wreckage of the battlefield, pulling parts from a smashed rifle and rummaging through a discarded backpack. But she was careful not to wrong the dead by stealing from them and always said a prayer when a body lay nearby.

Soon, Devi came upon an artillery pond that seemed a strange kind of oasis, where a few ducks floated, unperturbed by the death and decay all around them. Devi kneeled at the water's edge and looked around, before unbuttoning her shirt. She discarded the length of fabric she used to bind her chest and examined her red skin chafed raw. From her pocket, she removed Arjuna's red and yellow kerchief and used it to wash her body, her bare breasts exposed.

It was the closest she could get to her womanhood. That and the nurses at the Canadian casualty clearing station behind the frontline. The first time, she had carried a gravely wounded comrade on her shoulder all the way to the wooden barracks of the aid station. When she had opened the door, Devi miraculously entered a world filled with female nurses in pressed blue uniforms and white veils, with pale determined faces, diligently tending to the wounded men. Before that moment, Devi had been alone for so long in the trenches—the only woman—that she had begun to think she was the only female left in the world.

She had felt a thrill seeing all those women at the field hospital followed by a feeling of desperate loneliness, sensing she had been cut off from her own womanhood. After that first visit, she returned at every opportunity, carrying wounded comrades to be treated by the Canadians. Inside the barracks, she would linger among the nurses just to be close to the sisterhood. And she never failed to secret away cotton gauze pads in her uniform to be used for her menstruation.

Hundreds of yards from where Devi now bathed, an impossibly tall soldier stood at the lip of the German trench, watching something through his binoculars. He put them down, shocked. "They've got women fighting," he said.

"Bull," said a soldier brandishing a Mauser G98 sniper rifle.

The sniper moved into position beside the tall soldier to take a closer look. As he stared down the scope of his rifle, he saw her, too, and his jaw went slack. "A female Gurkha. Remarkable."

He brought his rifle down, and for a moment the two soldiers marvelled in silence at this most strange, poetic sight. The sniper then made the sign of the cross and raised his rifle.

"War doesn't wait for any man *or woman*," he said, as he clunked a bullet into the chamber with a sharp tug of the bolt.

As the sniper rested a finger on the trigger, his compatriot seemed troubled. Then, as he fired the Mauser, the tall German nudged the long barrel of the rifle. The bullet cut through the air and harmlessly shot up a poof of dirt a few hundred yards away.

"What the hell!"

"Let her have some peace. We'll all be dead soon enough."

*

When Devi had finished washing herself, she tightly rewrapped her chest with the fabric and began the dangerous journey back toward British lines, collecting bits of firewood and bowing to several crosses with German and French helmets perched on top. She stopped at the edge of another flooded artillery crater. Around her reflection was half-submerged debris, animal carcasses, and several bodies floating face down. Then, amid the deathly decay, she saw a single pristine flower, which brought her a measure of joy.

Minutes later, Devi leapt into the trench, her uniform bulging. Startled, Badri fell backward, fearing a sneak attack by the Germans. When he saw the firewood in Devi's hands, he scoffed, "Collecting firewood! Isn't that a woman's work?"

Devi had a thousand cutting responses but said nothing.

At the same time, Captain Hughes moved down the trench distributing letters to the soldiers of his company. He handed a letter to Arjuna then approached Devi. He looked regretfully at her and showed an empty hand, before continuing down the trench.

Devi unpacked extra rations and spare parts from inside her uniform. The Gurkhas gathered around, clearly impressed—all but Badri, who always seemed to find fault with her. Devi handed one soldier the parts he needed for his rifle. Next, she handed the Gurkha soldier with the broken compass a new one.

He looked down at the compass and pointed south-east. "Home is that way!"

"4,000 miles *THAT WAY*," added Rakesh.

Devi handed Pukuli's father a tin of food. "From what world have you been sent," he said, appreciatively.

She held out the pristine flower from the pond to Arjuna. Someone whistled in response to the gesture. Arjuna backed away from the flower, uncertain of its meaning.

When Devi eyed his make-shift altar, Arjuna finally understood and placed the flower in his altar as an offering.

Devi paused a moment, as if considering whether it was the right moment. Then she fished out an ornate garland made with the safety pins from the field dressing kits she had been collecting.

Arjuna grinned ear to ear as he took possession of the necklace, another gift he hoped would please the gods. He bowed to Devi with joined palms then found a spot on the ground to sit. There, he sliced open the envelope with his kukri and unfolded the letter given to him by his captain.

In the near distance, the British troops continued to drink and merry-make, among them Corporal Smith.

From inside her jacket pocket, Devi withdrew several postcard-size images and stared at them, pensively.

Pukuli's father eyed Devi as he ate from his tin. She saw his gaze and passed him the images. Badri, with one hand tucked in his pants for comfort, witnessed the exchange. "Is that your woman? If only they could see us now. Ha! This is a *man's* world!"

"You're right," responded Devi. "No woman would have been foolish enough to create such a hell."

Pukuli's father regarded the images a long while until Badri impatiently reached for them.

"I'm starving without my family," said Pukuli's father then looked down at his tin of food, his appetite lost. He passed the images to another soldier, bypassing Badri. The soldier shuffled through the images.

"It's so flat here. I miss the mountains," said the soldier, before passing the images to Rakesh, ignoring Badri's reaching hands. "What's he doing with a picture of your mother?" Rakesh asked.

Badri had had enough and snatched the images away. The image in hand was that of the many-armed goddess, Kali, wearing a girdle of severed arms and a necklace of skulls. Her tongue dripped blood.

Laughter rose among the Gurkhas, and Devi allowed herself to smile quietly.

Arjuna looked up from his letter before turning his attention back to the page. All expression bled from his face.

Just then, a British private with a mouth full of broken teeth staggered among the Gurkhas. "What you Indians up to?"

"We're Gurkhas," said Devi.

"Yeah, Gurkhas," said the others from her unit.

A motley lot of British soldiers arrived behind the private. "You don't say!? It's Johnny Gurkha!"

"Ox holes," bellowed Rakesh at the pale faces.

Anwyl, Maddocks, Cadogan, and Hardie, who stood nearby, grew alert to the stand-off. Maddocks moved to step in, but Cadogan held him back. "The English are ugly today."

"Is that different from any other day?" replied Maddocks.

"Today, they are in the mood to be dangerous," warned Cadogan. "So maybe the Nepalese will keep the bloody English off our backs awhile."

The British began baiting the Gurkhas, nudging each other with every insult. "A tiny lot, ain't they boys?"

A rumble of approval.

"Makes us smaller targets for German bullets," said Pukuli's dad, dismissively.

"And we've got all our teeth!" called Rakesh, smiling with a mouth full of bright white teeth.

The Gurkhas had their turn to snicker. All but Badri. "When you speak like that to the English, you bring our people down!" he said, in disgust. "Proves we aren't worthy, doesn't it?"

"Stop imitating the English, you twig of a man," said Rakesh, dismissively. "They still won't accept you any more than any of us."

"Listen, you savages," shouted the soldier with rotten teeth. "We *is* the greatest nation in the world, which makes you, well, a dog turd. If we wanted to, we could throw you lot in concentration camps like we did the damn Boers and negros back there in Africa."

"Who needs to pay a quid to go to the circus when we're surrounded by these swinish clowns," shouted Maddocks angrily at the British troops.

"Filthy Taffy," Corporal Smith shouted back, sloshed.

"No matter," grumbled Maddocks to his mates just loud enough for Smith to hear. "The good news is if this mound of useless flesh gets brain damaged by artillery, he may end up smarter than he is right now."

Smith stepped towards the Welsh, but his compatriots pulled him back. They felt invincible but weren't too drunk to know that a fight on two fronts was unwise, so they ignored the Welsh and focused on the under-class Nepali troops.

"Heard them knives is like boomerangs," the British soldier with rotted teeth said, in another attempt to taunt.

Rakesh moved to draw his knife. "Give it a whirl! The only thing you have to lose is your head."

"Is it true they gotta taste blood every time they's drawn?" persisted the British private.

Arjuna put down his letter and charged at the man with broken teeth, his eyes full of rage.

The private stumbled backward, tripping over his own feet. Other British soldiers advanced down the trench but were blocked by the Gurkhas with their kukris at the ready.

Devi pulled Arjuna back. "What's gotten into you?"

He roughly pulled his hand from her grip. "These people don't deserve our help. We should be home protecting *our* people."

"Yur just meat for the grinder. Nothing more," scoffed the drunken Englishman.

Devi shoved the private back toward the line of British soldiers. "Get lost!"

Captain Hughes approached Devi with books in his hand. Arjuna pushed past his commanding officer and fell to his knees praying and vigorously prostrating himself before his altar.

Staring down the English, Hughes barked, "If we fight each other like this, we'll never win this ruddy war. Remember—they are fighting our war, not the other way around."

The British soldiers sheepishly backed away down the trench.

Under his breath, Corporal Smith cursed Hughes. "Goddamn sheep-shaggin'—"

"—Another peep from you, and I'll send you to the Germans, you drunken fool."

Captain Hughes turned his attention to Devi. "I apologize for the fuss. For all their talk of being the most civilized nation in the world. Well, they sometimes act like downright barbarians." He collected his thoughts, then continued: "Listen private. I know you resent us bringing you here."

"The gods forged our people to protect the earth from demons." Devi gestured to the corpses, the wounded, and the resting soldiers. "But there're no demons here. Just men. Hungry and frightened, suffering and dying."

In the near distance, Arjuna prayed. He glanced over, sorrowfully.

Captain Hughes caught sight of the image in Devi's hand. She passed him the imprint of the goddess Devi. "She holds the entire universe in her womb," explained Devi, clasping her belly.

Arjuna looked at her strangely, and Devi immediately released her hands from the maternal gesture. "She protects us, as we protect our people."

As Colonel Young strode toward him, Captain Hughes immediately stood erect and saluted.

"Movement on the German lines. Mobilize your men immediately!"

Captain Hughes turned back to Devi. "I'd like to know more about these things." He handed her back the image of Devi, the goddess. "Until then, I pray she shields us from harm."

Devi bowed before saluting. Captain Hughes followed Young away down the trench.

In just a few minutes, a bagpiper's tune began to haunt the front lines. Devi walked through the snaking trench filled with tired looking Gurkhas. Artillery fell at an increasing rate. "It's time!"

The Gurkhas collected themselves for battle, as Devi moved to Arjuna kneeling at the bottom of the trench. "We've got to get ready."

He didn't move.

"Arjuna."

Arjuna held up the letter, his eyes full of tears. "I'm an orphan," he moaned.

"*Athma le santi milos*," she responded, resting a hand on his shoulder. "May your father's soul find peace."

## GURKHA

Devi made haste and prepared for the fight ahead.

# LAST BREATH

In the upper reaches of a wedge-shaped valley above Dharma's village, the old man sat on a glacier bare-chested wearing nothing but a loin cloth. His breathing was deep and explosive, and it appeared something terrible was happening to him from the inside. Yet his expression remained calm, the skin of his body glowing red. All around him, small pools of water formed under his heated body, which seemed to defy the glacier's frigid temperatures.

Only as he finished meditating did Dharma slowly open his eyes. Rising behind him were towering seracs of blue ice, while yawning crevasses criss-crossed the massive glacier. The lands surrounding Mahisha's kingdom on the distant slopes appeared to smoulder, with fiery embers belching from the cracks in the earth.

In the weeks that followed, Dharma trained in martial arts with renewed vigour, tended his fields, and thought often about the village men who had gone off to fight in a foreign land as he once had. Many, he imagined, would never return home alive. He reflected on his past, of joys and regrets, and of the mysterious young man, Dev, who had shown up just before Mahisha's return to the valley.

Then, one evening, as he sat by the fireplace at his home, reading the sacred text, the *Bhagavad Gita*, a darkness swept over the room. Dharma looked to the doorway.

"Where is she?" said the demon from the shadows.

Dharma pointed to his beloved wife's red dress that he had pulled from the trunk the previous week on the anniversary of their marriage in Bhaktapur. "I should ask the same," he called back to the *asura*.

Mahisha pointed to his stomach. "She awaits you."

Dharma glanced out into the darkness and could see Mahisha's eyes peering out from the cover of forest.

With lightning speed, Dharma whipped a knife at the demon, but Mahisha was already gone.

The old man knew it was time and dressed in a clean white shirt and a long shamanic skirt. He stepped before a cracked mirror on the wall, facing himself. For a time, he stared deeply, intrigued how his old age, like some sort of wrinkled mask, concealed the youth of his past.

Dharma carefully placed protective necklaces of black seed and snake vertebrae around his neck then crowned himself with a headdress of peacock feathers and porcupine quills. He glanced toward the iron weapons in the corner of the room—spears, swords, crescent-shaped blades.

For hours, Dharma prayed at the altar, uttering the mantra *OM*, the sound reverberating through his body and soul.

At nearly the same moment, Devi sat in the muddy trench studying the kukri given to her by Dharma. Behind her, several soldiers hauled dead Germans to the top of the trench to use as human sandbags.

As artillery fell sporadically, Devi thought she heard Dharma's voice and called out to him by name.

Hughes soon gathered his troops and stood erect among them. "Boys, do you hear that?" he finally asked.

"The bombs?" queried one soldier.

"No, not the bombs. The voices singing."

Hughes wasn't troubled by the puzzled looks of his men and took a moment to appreciate the unshaven faces staring out from behind the layers of dirt and grime, their bright eyes still holding so much life. "All of you in this trench today are one nation—singing with one voice. Let's sing a song full of hope," continued Hughes, his voice rising and falling, musically. "Let's sing a song of courage on the path to victory. A song that will be heard as far away as the green hills of our beloved homeland. And when the Germans come knocking—and they will come knocking—let's open the door gladly. Let's swing the door open wide for them, boys! And to the Germans we will sing in one voice, *welcome to hell*! Let us show them some real Welsh and English and Nepali hellfire...from the barrels of our guns and the points of our knives! And let's do it gladly with a smile!"

"A rousing speech from our commander!" said Hardie, impressed. "I've never heard him sound more Welsh in my life!"

A ripple of laughter eased the tension in the trench.

Hughes snapped a salute to his fellow soldiers and officers. "To you, I say thank you. Thank you for your service. Thank you for your sacrifice." He bowed his head a moment to stymie a flash of emotion. "I say this with all of my heart. It has been the greatest honour of my life to serve as your commanding officer. Godspeed, one and all."

That's when the French reinforcements arrived from the reserve trenches at the rear, soon followed by Canadian troops. They were dirty and battle hardened. Among them, a slight man with skin like Devi's, jumped silently into the trench, wearing suede moccasins on his feet. A beaded medicine bag hung across his shoulder alongside his Ross rifle.

He and Devi met eyes. Something powerful united them.

Devi bowed. "Namaste."

"*Aaniin*," the man said softly, before slipping away, disappearing into the knot of amassing troops.

Devi turned to see Captain Hughes watching, mightily impressed. "Who was that?" she asked.

"Private Francis Pegahmagabow," said Hughes. "Of the Ojibwa peoples. A Canadian sniper of the first order."

*

An evening mist clung low in Dharma's valley. The thundering of Mahisha's footsteps rang but could not be seen. *Boom! Boom! Boom!* Wearing a shaman's mask, Dharma lay on his stomach, peering down on the valley, his collection of weapons at his side. Mahisha's booming footsteps grew louder. Dharma bolted, leaving behind all his weapons but for Devi's kukri.

In flashes, Devi saw Dharma preparing for battle, as she awaited orders with the other soldiers of her company at the bottom the trench. Her face remained tense with worry. Then she remembered her mother smiling, even when she had troubles. A vision came to her of the Buddha, the ninth avatar of the god Vishnu, an ever-present crescent smile on his lips. *Was he smiling because he was content or content because he was smiling?* She wondered. Devi suspected it was both.

Several artillery shells landed near the British lines but did not explode. They made only a dull thud on impact. "Jerry is sending their duds," called a British soldier. "Suppose that's a good thing for us!"

Their relief was ever so brief, as more hollow thuds landed around them. This sent a nervous wave over the Gurkhas, who were pressed against the trench wall ready to go over the top. A wind from the enemy lines brought with it a greenish-yellow swamp fog that swept down the lip of the trench.

Someone beside Devi coughed. Almost immediately, there was more coughing up and down the trench. Now retching.

Several soldiers passed out, convulsing and foaming at the mouth. Devi felt the burning in her throat then the coughing began. She looked to Arjuna, confused.

Panicked French soldiers retreated en masse out the back of the trench.

Captain Hughes turned to his men. "HOLD THE LINE!" he screamed.

Further down the trench, Canadian and Belgian soldiers appeared to hold their crotches with great intention.

Realizing the dire situation, Captain Hughes turned to his men and yelled, "Pee! Pee on a sock!"

There was mass confusion, as Gurkha and Welsh soldiers yanked off their boots to remove their socks. Arjuna fumbled to get inside his pants. The coughing and retching came to a feverish pitch. Arjuna relieved himself on a wool sock then yelled at Devi: "Do it! Do it now, Dev!"

"I can't!"

Arjuna reached out to undo Devi's pants, but she smacked his hand away. Again, he tried to get down her pants but was met with a driving elbow. With nothing else to do, he pressed his dripping urine-soaked sock to her nose.

She breathed in.

Desperately, Arjuna looked for something. Devi dove into her pocket and stuffed his cherished red and yellow kerchief into his hand.

He looked panicked, as he tried to urinate on it—but his bladder was empty and now he was close to passing out. Devi snatched his kerchief back and jammed it down her pants to pee on it. She put it to his nose and mouth and commanded for him to breathe in.

Wearing a protective mask against the chlorine gas, Colonel Young stepped from the bunker. He lifted the mask and blew his shrill whistle.

Captain Hughes signaled his men forward. "Let's get them! Before they finish us!"

"FOR THE GLORY OF THE EMPIRE!" cried a British soldier.

Pukuli's father saw it differently. He wasn't fighting for the glory of any country or empire—but so he could stay alive long enough to see his wife and daughter again. With that thought, he scrambled out of the trench toward enemy lines.

In unison, the other Gurkhas charged from the trench through the iridescent fog with kukris in one hand and guns in the other. Captain Hughes launched after them.

A whizzing bullet struck Private Maddocks in the chest as he went over the top. He collapsed into the trench, limp as a rag doll.

Not far away, Lieutenant Anwyl hid among the dead and dying.

As Devi and the other Gurkhas charged through smoke and fire, Dharma sped downhill toward the valley floor. He moved swiftly and shadow-like up behind Mahisha, who appeared in the mist as a thorny-fleshed bear, his black snout wet with frothy pus. Mahisha turned and grinned, knowingly.

The Gurkhas kept far apart as they ran through no-man's-land, while the Welsh soldiers raced up from behind. As the Gurkhas charged forward, they became silhouettes against the smoke and flame of battle.

"Ayo Gurkhali!" screamed Devi.

"Ayo Gurkhali!" the other Gurkhas hollered.

The Welsh wailed their own battle cry, which somehow gave them courage.

Several soldiers running alongside Devi were mowed down by heavy gunfire. Another was blown to rags by falling artillery. Through the wreckage of the battlefield, Devi charged forward, leaping over barbed wire. It felt to her that she was a horse at full gallop. Up ahead, a cliff was fast approaching, and she could do nothing to change her destiny. She knew she was going over the edge.

More of Devi's compatriots were cut down in a hail of bullets. Behind her, Rakesh got snagged by barbed wire. He howled.

Badri turned around and raced toward Rakesh, as if coming to his aid, but kept sprinting toward the allied trenches. A bomb went off before him. He thought twice and doubled back toward the enemy trench.

As Private Cadogan sprinted onward, a bullet struck him in the eye, and his sight went black. Then all his thoughts slipped into darkness, too.

Pukuli's father raced bravely in front of Devi but vanished in the flame of an explosion. Devi's soul filled with rage. The world was ending before her eyes, and it was too late to change fate.

Another burst, and Private Hardie was blown back.

The German trench was just ahead. The tall soldier who had seen Devi bathing in no-man's-land peered above the lip of the trench.

"They're coming!" he screamed back to his compatriots. "Run for your lives!"

But there was no reaction from the other soldiers. Now he screamed, "G-U-R-K-H-A-S!"

All at once, terror struck the trench. En masse, weapons were dropped and the Germans fled.

The Himalayas shimmered in a cold blue light. Wearing the shaman's mask, Dharma was face to face with Mahisha.

"To the gods, repent," said Dharma.

Mahisha swiped the mask off Dharma's face. "Why? When soon I'll be a god!"

"It's not too late to change."

"You, old man, are the one who never changes."

Dharma flew at Mahisha, Devi's rusted kukri in hand. The movement of his knife left trails of circular light, which bent in the presence of the shape-shifting demon.

"Where have you been hiding her?" demanded Mahisha.

Dharma did not speak.

"MY BRIDE!"

In that instant, it occurred to Dharma the true identity of the child he had spent months living with and training. He marveled at his own blindness at what had been in front of him the whole time.

"Where's my bride?" Mahisha bellowed, impatiently.

Dharma smiled, satisfied. "Where she can't be found."

With an open palm, Dharma applied pressure to Mahisha that defied physical contact and threw Mahisha off balance. He slashed Mahisha with Devi's kukri. Mahisha was surprised by the gaping wound. "What powers this kukri possesses."

"Did I not teach you anything? Magic is what we bring to the world." Dharma flew at Mahisha with the point of the kukri. In constant fluid motion, Dharma moved around Mahisha. Their movements appear unified in a dance of light and darkness.

Back in the British trench, polished boots arrived before Lieutenant Anwyl, who was cowering among the dead. Colonel Young lorded above. "You cowardly Taff. Go fight the Jerries or die right here."

Anwyl was too paralyzed by fear to move or speak, his mind plagued by terrible thoughts of pain and a gruesome death.

Colonel Young stood above Anwyl, his pistol now pointed at the lieutenant. "Well? One last chance."

Anwyl remained stuck in place like a fly in ointment. "I can't-can't move, sir. My legs, they won't move."

"Okay," said the colonel, in a conciliary tone. "I will take care of this."

"Really? Thank you, sir. Next time, I will try harder, I will."

"I'm sure." The colonel managed a smile before pulling the trigger.

The bullet cut clean through Anwyl's beating heart. His frightened eyes sprung wide in disbelief. The young Welshman slumped over, dead.

"War can't be won by cowards," Young muttered, as he went off in search of other traitors.

Nearby, Private Maddocks, blood-soaked and gravely wounded, watched with horror, as Anwyl was murdered at the colonel's feet.

*

Devi, Captain Hughes, and the remaining Gurkhas stormed the German trench, which had been abandoned but for the wounded and dead. Several Gurkhas shouted in victory. Devi looked around, seething. "The Huns show us no mercy! *We'll show them our knives!*"

She stormed past a German fighter who appeared dead among the bodies littering the trench. Devi tracked a wounded German dragging himself away, his pant legs shredded, his flesh riddled with shrapnel. One-handed, she aimed her carabine at his head, her other hand gripping Dharma's kukri.

He looked back to her, pleading. "I beg you," he said, in broken English, suddenly recognizing Devi.

Devi rested her finger on the trigger.

"Wait!" he shouted. "I showed you mercy. At the pond. When you were bathing. I swear on the life of my family."

Devi hesitated, her mouth agape. He was the only one who knew her true identity. Still, she couldn't bring herself to kill someone so close to death. She lowered her weapon, which brought relief to the soldier.

"It's destiny that we meet again," he said, grateful.

"Fate is written here," she said, pointing to her forehead.

The tall soldier touched his forehead, marvelling at the thought. Then a whistling sound as an artillery strike obliterated the ground where only seconds before he had touched his fate. Devi was thrown up against the trench wall by the blast, her sight temporarily lost, her ears ringing terribly.

Behind her, the German fighter who had appeared dead, as he bided his time, came back to life. He kicked the kukri from her hand, which flew down the trench.

He lunged for it.

Another soldier with a long hunting knife leapt down on Devi. She turned and immediately struck his elbow with the butt of her rifle, and the knife released from his grip. Next Devi cracked his collar bone and jabbed him in the stomach, sending the soldier doubling over, winded. Devi butted him in the head and twisted his hand so that he spun his back to her in agony.

Using the rifle butt in the small of the soldier's back, she manipulated him toward the German fighter, who ripped off his shirt, revealing a stained undershirt and bulging muscles. The German fighter cut back and forth with Dharma's knife, while Devi used the captured soldier as a shield.

The German fighter dodged the other soldier, but, impatient with the game of cat and mouse, roughly shoved aside his fellow soldier, removing the obstacle in his path.

Devi pummeled the German fighter, but he quickly overpowered her and straddled her on the ground, pressing the kukri toward her heart. Devi struggled to off-set his balance, but he was too strong. The point of the knife pushed against her, piercing the fabric of her shirt. A growing stain of blood soaked through.

"Watch out!" shouted Arjuna.

A soldier at the top of the trench pointed his rifle down at Devi. Arjuna tackled the soldier, as he fired.

Devi slipped out from under the German and twisted the kukri upward so that the fighter's own pressing weight sunk deep onto the curved point of the blade.

He slumped over.

Across space but not time, Dharma pushed on with his fight against Mahisha. The demon's fleshy body was covered in knife wounds.

"Love wounds hate," said Dharma.

Mahisha grinned at his lacerated flesh. "And such love you show!" In that moment, the beast seemed to summon an unearthly energy and grew in size.

The demon slammed Dharma, who took control of his fall.

With his newfound strength, Mahisha squeezed the old man's knife hand, snapping his arm like a dry twig. He groaned in agony, his arm limp.

Human figures pushed out on Mahisha's membrane-like flesh from within. A hand. A foot. A face, screaming.

"I raised you to embrace all things," pleaded Dharma. "But *you* squeeze the soul out of *everything*."

"Even you!"

A series of shells exploded near Arjuna and Devi, blowing debris over the German trench.

"Those are British shells!" she shouted, gripping Dharma's kukri, which—magical or not—simply couldn't protect them against the sinister devices of war. She had promised Arjuna's father to protect him, but there was regretfully nothing left she could do. Arjuna's father was dead. They, too, would be dead soon enough. Only the demon, Mahisha, would be left to live on, haunting the earth for all eternity.

As Captain Hughes approached, Devi heard the sound of an incoming shell. She had a feeling about this one and shoved Arjuna and Hughes out of its path. A blinding flash. Silence. And a loud roar, as the artillery round spat fire and debris.

Minutes on the battlefield passed like hours, but, in time, the ferocity of combat abated, and the field of war fell quiet. Both sides tended to their countless dead and wounded.

From above, Devi appeared dead among the wreckage, Dharma's kukri cradled loosely in her hand.

At the edge of a smoking crater, Arjuna stared out at no-man's-land. Behind him stood Captain Hughes. "I'm afraid Dev is gone—*forever*."

Arjuna refused to accept that and darted into no-mans-land.

Private Hardie, the left side of his face torched, his clothes blown to rags, staggered before Captain Hughes. He saluted and collapsed. "Sir," gasped Hardie, as the captain tended to his wounds. "Lieutenant Anwyl. Is dead."

Captain Hughes struggled to bottle up the loss but he could no longer hide his grief.

Out in no-man's-land, a lone white horse wandered like an apparition through the carnage within view of Devi's body. Beside her knelt the god, Dhanwantari, blue-skinned and four-armed. In one hand he held herbs, another a golden cup. As he leaned over Devi and exhaled a golden light, Dharma lay prostrate beneath Mahisha's mighty jaws half a world away.

"How did I fail you this badly? We raised you as our own," said Dharma in defeat.

"I needed my father!" shouted the demon. "But you abandoned me. Like everyone else."

"I joined the British to give you and your mother a better life."

"You never understood what I needed! And now I will take what's mine. That girl!" Mahisha raised his claw. "Then immortality!"

As Dharma's vision was eclipsed by Mahisha's mighty jaws, the old man took one final breath and uttered *OM*, thinking of Brahman, the great Lord, the Supreme. For a single instant, he envisioned Devi, hoping upon hope she would make it back from the war alive. All at once, Dharma's world went dark and silent.

Mahisha rose up on hind legs, his face bloody. Angry and confused, he turned toward the heavens and hollered. His hunger remained unsatiated, and the death of Dharma had done nothing to lift the weight from his burdened soul.

Mahisha's haunted howl echoed over no-man's-land.

Devi gasped awake. "Dharma!"

She collapsed, letting go of Dharma's kukri.

Arjuna heard the shout then spotted Devi among the wreckage. He raced to her side. "Medic!" he hollered, as he cradled her head in his lap.

At her side, the kukri lay in the dirt. Arjuna picked up the knife and gently guided it into its sheath.

# CYCLE

# II

*People become great because of their heart not their caste*
Nepali Proverb

# KINGDOM OF FIRE

In the distance, a company of Gurkha soldiers marched up the valley toward Dharma's village. Beyond the lower slopes, Mahisha's kingdom had grown in their absence, with scaffolding made of bones and strapped together with sinew and the stringy cords of intestines. Several neighbouring summits were blackened, scorched by the demon's ungodly fires. It was as if the demon's strength had been fortified by feasting on the sorrow of humans, engorged on their misery and pain. Beyond Mahisha's reach, the snowy spindrift blew sideways off the highest summits like smoke signals pleading to the gods.

The returning Gurkhas marched up the stone steps, exhausted from the long journey on foot from the lowlands. Several maimed veterans were carried in giant baskets strapped to men's backs, while Devi and Arjuna assisted Rakesh, who was missing his left leg below the knee.

Rakesh gazed toward his beloved Himalayas then closed his eyes and took a deep breath. "I was afraid I'd never get to breathe this air again."

"And now that we've been demobilized, we never have to leave here again," said Arjuna.

"Good thing you made corporal, and I was promoted to private first class. It should come with a tidy pension that we can use to help the village," said Rakesh, as he limped on.

Arjuna looked to Devi, bitterly. "But what did Dev get for all his bravery?"

The other Gurkhas shook their heads, gravely.

"Nothing. No promotion, no pay raise."

"It's okay," she said.

Arjuna couldn't let it go. "Even that human sandbag, Smith, made sergeant!"

"Is it true Hughes recommended you be awarded the Victoria Cross for your heroism in battle, but Young denied it?" asked Rakesh.

"The colonel is a vindictive muck," Arjuna fumed. "I don't understand why he despises Dev so much."

"It doesn't matter, Arjuna," she said, as she glanced around at their sparse numbers. Where once a thousand men had marched off to war, now only two hundred broken souls returned. She whispered a prayer for all those no longer with them.

For her, it felt like a lifetime ago, a past life, that this place existed beyond a shadow of memory. It had been buried deep in the muddy trenches of Belgium, too painful to recollect. Now she could feel Dharma's presence in every view, in every stone step she climbed. His imprint in the landscape was undeniable, and she took comfort in that.

Among the Gurkhas marched a platoon of British and Welsh soldiers.

"*Dyna harddwch*," said Private Hardie in Welsh, as he admired the towering mountains all around.

"*Ie. There is beautiful*, indeed," responded Cadogan.

Hardie turned to Cadogan, revealing a terrible burn on half his face. Cadogan wore a patch over the eye lost to a German bullet so that he resembled a blue-eyed pirate.

"It ain't Conwy," said Cadogan. "And for now, that's a good thing."

"No matter," responded Hardie. "We go where they pay us to go."

"You can say what you want," said Cadogan. "But I will tell you this. I ain't going home, you hear me? Not yet. Maybe never, even." What he knew was that the war had scrambled his mind terribly. There were no words to describe the horror, the comradery, the loss, and he had no interest speaking of it to anyone who hadn't been there.

"What next then? And why did they send us back here?" asked another soldier.

"O," said Hardie. "I think our special mission is to find more hillmen for the British. Why else would Young be stationed in Mumbai, and we're stuck here with his flat-faced bulldog, Smith."

Cadogan waved away Hardie like he was old French cheese. "Say no more, boy. I don't wanna hear another word of this," he protested.

Directly behind, Hughes huffed with each step climbed.

"Well, perhaps the gravity of being promoted to major is weighing you down," chided Hardie.

"Or perhaps we're no longer in the flats of Belgium," he responded, brightly. "At least there's none of this Spanish Flu business up here. What do you say, Maddocks?"

Private Maddocks walked alone, looking troubled like he wanted to hurt someone. The war had turned his mop of black hair white. He ignored Hughes and ignored the pain from the bullet fragments lodged in his chest from the frontlines. His body may have survived, but he felt as dead as any of the corpses left to rot on the battlefield.

As the group arrived in the village, locals lined the path, bowing to the procession. Several houses appeared to have been knocked over by a tremendous wind. A woman fixed a roof, while another worked the iron forge.

Several Gurkhas grumbled in disapproval at the women doing a *man's work*.

The young girl, Pukuli, had grown since the village men had left for the war years before. The young teen called to the passing soldiers, her voice full of hope. "Papa? Have you seen papa?"

Badri avoided the girl's probing eyes.

Pukuli saw Devi, and her eyes lit up. "Where's *bubah*?"

Devi looked to her, sadly. Pukuli's expression immediately fell, her hopes dashed, and she ran away in tears.

\*

That night, the sun fell behind the Himalayas, and the valley went dark.

Inside Dharma's hut, a lamp flickered on the table. Devi stood before the old, cracked mirror, her reflection fractured. She studied herself and grew emotional. "I mustn't cry," she whispered to herself.

She thought of the last dinner she had as a little girl with her mother and father, eating *dhido* and *gundruk ko zhol* around the little round table on the floor. And how her dad had a tip of rice wine and soon was red-faced and laughing and talking more than usual, the weight of their difficult lives, for a time, lifted from his shoulders. Reaching across the table, he had touched Devi's cheek, affectionately, and it was like there were only three people left in the world, and she was perfectly happy about it.

"I mustn't cry," she again whispered to her reflection.

As night after night fell, Devi sat in the darkness dressed in her military uniform, staring at the barren field, deeply troubled. She used Dharma's kukri to cut off her hair in mourning. Each night, the distant sound of war echoed—artillery, bagpipes, the faint cry of men cut down in battle. "Without love, even the power of the greatest god is blind," she heard Dharma say. Devi's eyes were full of torment. "And when the truth can't be seen...we become only shadows of ourselves, unleashing demons."

"Enough, Dharma! Enough!" she shouted at the night.

Devi hung her head in defeat and didn't stir until the light gathered on the horizon. A brisk wind suddenly sounded through the trees like bamboo chimes. She gazed up at the fallow field and saw something she hadn't previously noticed.

The morning light soon revealed Devi barefoot, using a wooden implement to churn the earth. And in the days that followed, Devi planted the field and brought up water from the river to feed Dharma's land. It was the least she could do for the man who had given her a second life, despite his own resistance at the beginning.

In the evening, flames danced in the fire pit, as several pots bubbled and steamed. Devi had remained in uniform all these months, not yet ready to forget the past. She unbuckled her belt and removed the sheathed kukri that Dharma had said was magic. But she saw no magic in the deadly weapon and carefully wrapped it in cloth and placed it in Dharma's trunk alongside the red dress. Then she stepped outside to escape the interior heavy with memories.

The mountains hung high above Dharma's hut, and she found herself a spot on a rock where she contemplated something burning in the distance. Only as she focused did she see that it was a small hillside village in flames. She knew who had done it and turned her gaze toward Mahisha's blackened castle.

For many weeks, she made the trip up and down to the river hundreds of times. The neighbours avoided looking at the strange war veteran who lived silent and alone on the hill, her clothes filthy, her eyes always fixed somewhere beyond this world.

As Devi tended her field, she would kneel and closely examine the ground for some sign of life, but there was only dirt.

She persisted with her efforts. And, always, she found comfort with the elemental feel of the soft moist earth underfoot and in her hands and fingers that dug and prodded the land, coaxing it to life.

One morning, after a night of rain, she lay on her bed of straw and felt hopeless. The field would not grow. She knew she killed everything she loved, even the seeds she had planted.

But as she stepped outside into the sunshine, she saw it. A tiny plant pushed up through the earth. Upon closer examination, the entire field of plants had pushed miraculously above the surface.

She laughed and lay down, resting her head by the small plants. She closed her eyes and immediately fell into a deep sleep.

*

It was impossible to say how long Devi had been up there alone, but the plants that had once only been seeds were now shoulder height. With absolute love and devotion, Devi tended to her fields, as if they were children, humming the melody her mother once sang. And with the summer growing season now coming to its end, she would harvest her fields with the same care and respect.

One day, when her work was done, she began the somber task of organizing Dharma's possessions, though she avoided opening his British East India trunk. Some items she would keep, like the candlesticks for pujas, while others she would give away. Among his things, she found a copy of the sacred *Bhagavad Gita*, the Song of God. Dharma had told her that the *Gita* was not a philosophical text but a devotional one, guiding readers to enlightenment.

Devi wasn't much of a reader, having only learned a little from Dharma when he was alive. Still, she needed to find a source of strength and opened the book, using a finger to slowly track her progress down the page.

Several times, Dharma had warned her about losing sight of God, as he had done himself in the past. "When you forget the Supreme Brahman," he had told her, "you start to think that the material world you see with your eyes is the only reality. When it's only a fragment of a much greater reality. Then you are destined to be trapped in *maya*, illusion, and *samsara*, continuously being born, dying and being reborn and never reaching that blessed state, nirvana. Eternity, my Dev, dwells in the soul."

A rustling in the bushes stole her attention. But it wasn't a demon that came into view. It was Arjuna still dressed in uniform.

"Just checking in on a dear comrade," he said, with a friendly military salute.

Devi paused, staring. She had not spoken to anyone in months, and it felt as if her tongue had been cut off and her lips sewn shut.

She forced the words out, "Food?"

He pointed to his belly and affirmed his hunger.

Soon Devi and Arjuna were sitting on a rock in Dharma's field, silently eating from bowls. Arjuna wore a t-shirt, his military jacket folded neatly beside him.

She watched him from the corner of her eye, as his muscular biceps flexed as he ate. She loved the shape of his eyes and the curve of his lips.

"You've become a man," she offered.

Arjuna looked down at the bowl of food, satisfied. "And you, my friend, are as skilled in the kitchen as you are on the battlefield."

Devi's cheeks flushed. "I'm glad you're here."

"Then we're both glad."

He regarded her field with interest. "I'm impressed. You got this land to yield more than Dharma ever could."

This made Devi smile.

"But I do think it's time you reap what you've sown. The rice harvest is already underway in the lower valley."

She acknowledged his words but couldn't help but feel criticized.

"So how have you been, Dev?" he asked, trying to keep his friend from receding back inward.

"Have you ever almost drowned?"

Arjuna nodded in the affirmative and held up three fingers.

"It's an awful feeling, reaching for the bottom with your toes only to realize there's no bottom—so you keep sinking."

"We've all been at the bottom so long. We need to come up for air."

Arjuna paused and looked out over the vast landscape. The upper valley leading to Mahisha's kingdom was black. Light and colour warped around the demon's fortress. Fissures in the earth bubbled with molten fire. "You know, while you take care of your fields, *he* gets stronger."

"Perhaps Mahisha isn't the only demon we need to fear. Maybe it's the British Empire. Or maybe, Arjuna, it's us." She couldn't speak. "We took so many lives."

"I know, Dev. I know. But if we don't defend ourselves against Mahisha, then we all die."

Arjuna noticed something at her waist.

She tracked his gaze to the place where her kukri had always been secured. "No more, Arjuna. I'm done with weapons."

"You can't be serious!"

"On my life, I swear it."

"But the demon killed your parents and Dharma—and my father and brother!"

Arjuna could see he wasn't getting through. "Believe me, I understand why you don't want to fight anymore. But with the right understanding, the right perception, Dev, you don't need to renounce action. Only the desire for the outcome. *Nishkama Karma*," he offered. "Acting without desire."

She tilted her head in disagreement.

Arjuna wanted to protest but recognized he was a guest at Dev's home and didn't want to spoil the peace they shared, especially given Dev's reclusive state.

"Arjuna, why is it that we both lost parents, but because my mom lived and my father died, I got treated like mud. When your mom died, did people treat you differently?"

"No point dwelling on it."

"But were you shunned by the village?" she persisted. "Told you brought bad luck? My mother was expected to kill herself, throw herself on my father's funeral pyre to save her honour. But she resisted the village and was cast out for choosing to live and raise me."

He shook his head. "The world is unfair."

"That's not good enough. Do you believe we can change?"

His answer was too complicated to express, so he fell silent and gazed back to her fields. He sighed in resignation then rose to his feet, walking between the rows of crops.

And so it was, in the golden light of dusk, that Devi and Arjuna worked together to harvest her produce.

"You know," said Arjuna, finally. "From the moment I met you, I knew you were special. Just like your mother always said."

Devi looked away, concealing a joyful smile.

"But being alone so much isn't healthy."

Devi's smile faded. "It's getting late, Arjuna. You should go."

"There's a wedding party tonight. Come down to the village. With so many men lost, there're dozens of women to choose from."

"I should offer you the same advice."

"Despite everything, I want a wife. I want children," Arjuna persisted.

"So what do you want from me, then?" she said, full of anger and hurt.

Arjuna was perplexed by the question, so he bowed to her and backed away. "Get some rest, Dev. You're overtired."

Wordlessly, Devi watched Arjuna walk away down the dirt path. She already missed his presence.

# TRUNK OF MEMORIES

The stone-paved plaza was filled with colourful banners illuminated by brass oil lamps. Musicians played drums, hat-shaped bells, and a long-curved trumpet in preparation for the arrival of the bride and groom. Several children flew kites, which swooped back and forth across the sky like Griffon Vultures.

In one corner, a group of Welsh troops kept mostly to themselves drinking. One-eyed Cadogan raised his glass somberly in salutation. "To Anwyl. And all the others we done lost."

"True is it that we need to raise a battalion of hillmen for an action in Afghanistan?" asked Hardie.

"Don't speak that, boy," said Cadogan. "The guns haven't even cooled from Europe. Bloody empires and their endless appetites!" He licked his lips and waved for the bottle being passed around.

Hardie passed the bottle to Cadogan and said, "It would explain why the colonel is back."

"Hell," said Cadogan. "Colonel Young's back? So Smith, the flat-faced moron, is finally reunited with the moustached geezer?"

Maddocks, his mind elsewhere, heard this and immediately returned to the here and now. He looked up from cleaning his revolver, his eyes holding a demented light.

"Ya ain't saying much these days," Hardie said warily, addressing Maddocks.

"He hasn't been the same since *that* day," said Cadogan, as if Maddocks wasn't even among them.

"Is he ever gonna speak again?" queried Hardie.

Maddocks stayed silent.

Across the way, alcohol was poured into wood bowls among the elders. Major Hughes sat with them. They all wore Topi hats and had red tika smudged between their brows. In unison, they tipped their cups to the ground as a libation then drank.

They all made sour faces, while Major Hughes gagged and spat the rice wine in the dirt.

"In all the Himalayas, no one makes rice wine like my wife does!" said Mukhiya.

They rumbled in agreement.

At the edge of the square, Colonel Young stood with several British officers, including Sergeant Smith. He looked to Hughes with disdain. "Looks like our poor choirboy has gone native on us."

Before long, several people from a neighbouring village staggered through the bustling square, their clothes torn and singed by fire.

They arrived before the elders and bowed with joined palms.

"The demon burned our village to the ground. He's looking for a young woman. We brought all our women out but none was the one he sought."

The elders looked to one another, deeply concerned. All but Mukhiya. "Come back tomorrow," he said, dismissively. "As you can see, we are in the middle of a wedding celebration."

"But—"

The senior elder raised his hand to silence the villager, who shuffled away, rejected, along with the others.

The elder in white robes opened his mouth to speak but then thought otherwise.

"Is it not our way to make room for strangers in need?" hedged the elder with pockmarked skin.

"Am I not the Mukhiya, the village elder, a title I proudly carry as the oldest son of the previous Mukhiya—going back to the beginning of time?"

"Yes, yes," murmured the other elder, chastened. "But what is Mahisha's interest in this young woman?"

"My grandson is getting married today," said Mukhiya, curtly. "Mahisha can wait."

Soon a wedding song commenced, and the bride and groom arrived in a decorative basket carried on the shoulders of the villagers. Both wore colourful hand-woven grass garlands—a symbol of everlasting love—which were to be exchanged during the ceremony. The bride was dressed in red, while the groom wore a crisp white skirt. Mingled with the wedding guests, war amputees hobbled through the streets, still wearing their army uniforms.

Arjuna glanced up to Dharma's hut on the hill, disappointed.

Badri leaned against the wall, looking contemptuously toward the wedding.

As villagers danced around the bride and groom, throwing lotus petals, Devi walked into the plaza, quietly absorbing the festivities. She couldn't recall when last she had been present at such a large celebration, and she felt both the urge to laugh with joy and to flee back to the solitude of Dharma's hut.

When Rakesh, one-legged, saw her, his eyes lit up, and he bowed in deference to her. She returned the gesture.

Mukhiya caught sight of Devi and regarded her, critically, while Major Hughes nodded to her in acknowledgement.

She saluted back.

"I've never seen anyone fight more bravely," said Hughes, proudly, to the elders.

"This stranger has brought nothing but misfortune to the village," countered Mukhiya.

When Arjuna spotted Devi, he strode up to her, resting a hand on her shoulder. "You made it!"

She turned to see Arjuna accompanied by a beautiful woman, Uruwasi. The woman with fine features gushed over Arjuna, while his eyes remained fixed on Devi.

The serenity in Devi's expression vanished. She stalked away, leaving Arjuna dumbfounded. "Wait," he called after her. "You just got here!"

Devi stopped and turned back to Arjuna. "I can't do this anymore."

"Do what?"

"You'll find the truth at Dharma's hut."

Arjuna didn't look so sure.

With that, Devi escaped into the crowd.

Uruwasi sighed impatiently, uncertain why her future husband was so obsessed with the peculiar young man who kept to himself on the hill. "He's a strange one," she said.

"War can do that to a person," he offered.

"So can weddings."

*

The sun set over the terraced fields surrounding Dharma's hilltop home.

Devi stood in the doorway for a long while, lost. What was to be her life, she wondered. To tend plants alone? To eat alone? To sleep alone? To die alone?

She retreated inside.

As she surveyed the room—the sum of her remaining world—something pulled her back to the British East India trunk. By candlelight, she began to pull out some of the familiar objects she had previously seen, like the flintlock pistol and the silver flask with Dharma's name and rank engraved on it.

She went deeper and found old, faded images of Dharma with a woman photographed at a studio in Delhi, both dressed in their best attire. Though the photo was in black and white, Devi knew the woman was wearing the same red dress that she had found in the trunk.

At the very bottom of the trunk, she came upon something surprising. She pulled out a box and opened it up. Devi began to crank the handle on Dharma's machine with the small horn, which turned a black disc of music round and round. On the red label at the centre of the disc was written *Wolfgang Amadeus Mozart - Piano Concerto No. 21.*

ROBERT J. BRODEY

She had seen a gramophone once before behind the front lines in Europe and was no longer a total stranger to this miraculous technology. Perhaps had she never left her remote village, she would have thought it a demon speaking through the machine. But here and now, the music found its way inside her. She began to dance, as if possessed by the god of love herself. And something came over her, and the music guided her, inspired her to slip on the red dress.

She danced on, admiring her figure in the cracked mirror. For several long years, she had been a man, her true self buried beneath a disguise. But now she could resist no more and wanted to be a woman—for at least this moment.

Her shadow moved and spun through the doorway, dancing in the trees.

Arjuna burst through the doorway, drunk and holding up a jug of rice wine. "I know weddings can be..."

Arjuna looked up, shocked.

Devi, curved and beautiful in the fitted red dress, stopped dead, while Dharma's masks hung on the wall behind her bearing witness.

She felt dizzy with joy at seeing Arjuna, her secret finally revealed.

"—You!" is all he could say, recoiling at her sight.

"From the very beginning, I wanted to tell you. Now you see. I'm not Dev...I'm Devi."

"You...*demon!*"

Devi stepped toward him, knowing it would take a moment for him to process the truth.

He placed a hand on the handle of his kukri. "I trusted you with my life. And you betrayed me with this unthinkable deceit."

"Please," she said, patiently. She reached out and touched his cheek.

Arjuna slapped her hand away, violently. "What you've done has betrayed the gods themselves! They will strike you down if the villagers don't kill you first!"

Arjuna shoved her away, knocking the oil lamp off the table.

"Go back from where you came!" he shouted.

Despite his terrible words, she desperately wanted to hold him in place, to beg his understanding. Had they not shared a lifetime of experiences in just a handful of years? But Devi's courage failed her, and she watched silently as he stormed away.

Behind her, something glowed against the wall. She remained motionless as the flames grew higher. In seconds, the fire licked up the wall, consuming Dharma's shaman masks. Flames poured out of the eye and mouth holes like great angry spirits.

On the hilltop above the village, Dharma's house burned like a funeral pyre.

# THE RETURN

In a haze, Devi walked down the countless stone steps from Dharma's village, still wearing the red dress. She reached the valley floor then staggered across the swinging rope bridge strung over the thundering Kali Gandaki River. With each step, she withdrew further into the innermost compartment of her mind. Her mouth tasted of rot, fouled by her decomposing life. She rambled through the forest, unanchored from the world and thought only of death.

Soon she stopped before a sacred boulder painted long ago with the words:

LIFE IS A DREAM.
YOU ARE NOT DREAMING.

Through much of the night she hiked, not knowing where she was going but somehow always getting closer to the Hidden Valley, the valley of her birth. It began with the fire-burnt remains of birds, big and small, littered on the ground. Other animals, too, were caught up in the flash blaze—Himalayan foxes, deer, and the seared remains of the furry marmot that couldn't be saved by its underground burrow.

Then, up ahead, she saw her village. But it was not as she had left it or as she had imagined it these past years during her absence.

Charred and tattered prayer flags flapped. Village huts smouldered in ruins. Bodies were scattered like discarded corn husks after the harvest. Moaning from the buried and injured villagers sounded as if the earth itself was crying.

Devi stood amid the destruction and saw again the men engaged in hand-to-hand combat on the pitted battlefields of Belgium. The whooshing sound of incoming artillery. An explosion obliterated soldiers on both sides of the war, wasting them and scattering their remains in the most unnatural ways. But now, before her, it was not soldiers in uniform subjected to the abhorrent violence but rather children and older people and women and men who thought nothing of war.

Anish, the boy who had once followed Devi everywhere, stumbled overtop the flattened huts, searching for his mother. "Ama? Ama?" he cried.

Another villager, Birendra, with the crescent scar across his forehead, rose from the rubble, drenched in blood. He slowly focused. "Devi...Is that really you?"

She bowed.

"That demon, he won't stop...He's...He's looking for you."

"What would he want from me?" she asked, confounded.

"He says you are betrothed to him."

"Betrothed? Why would Mahisha want to marry me?"

Birendra could not answer that. "After you had disappeared—years ago—we'd heard rumours about you. But most of us thought you were dead, killed by the demon."

"Your return. It's a miraculous sign," said Anish's mother, her voice quaking, as she emerged through the drifting smoke. Anish ran to his mom, relieved.

Devi was taken aback. Anish's mother had had few kind words for Devi or her mother after her father died. But now, it seemed, she saw Devi in a new light.

Other villagers gathered around Devi, too.

"What are we going to do?" cried a villager.

"I'm sorry. I can't help," said Devi. "But I can take you to someone. Maybe he can protect you."

*

The pathways cutting through Dharma's village were strewn with bodies. Some villagers wandered the streets like ghosts—in a state of shock. Others helped the injured, bandaging them with lengths of fabric and splinting broken bones with sticks and twine.

As a house burned, several people worked desperately to put out the fire with buckets of water.

Wearing the red dress, Devi entered the plaza, followed by dozens of ragged villagers. Birendra stood by her side, still bathed in his own blood. Everyone stopped to stare at Devi. Some, like Rakesh, who was balanced on one leg with the support of a crutch, were in awe.

Others were aghast.

Uruwasi stepped to Devi, irate. "Your deceit did this! Marry that *asura*—to spare the village!" She looked to Arjuna for approval, but he was focused elsewhere, troubled. In that moment, she sensed she had lost him forever.

Villagers drew menacingly close to Devi.

Pukuli, Rakesh, and others blocked their advance but were pushed aside. One-legged, Rakesh tumbled.

Devi's villagers kindly helped Rakesh back up.

Badri drew his kukri and lunged at Devi, but she easily avoided his blow and sent him to the ground.

"Among these people, who can protect us?" asked Birendra in despair.

Without hesitation, Devi pointed to Arjuna.

As if shoved by an invisible hand, Arjuna stepped back.

Birendra looked to Devi, doubtful. "I'm afraid, you are our last hope."

"I made an oath of peace. To never pick up arms again."

Major Hughes, Cadogan, Hardie and the rest of the Welsh contingent appeared at the edge of the mob.

"What in god's green earth is going on!" Hughes demanded of the mob. At once, he saw Devi in the elegant red dress. "My word!"

Rakesh addressed the crowd. "We don't have much time. Mahisha will be back in the morning. With an entire army."

"Wouldn't it be best to retreat and live out our lives in peace elsewhere?" cried a villager.

"There's nowhere to hide. Mahisha won't rest until he gets what he wants," said Rakesh.

The entire village looked to Devi.

Mukhiya thrust an accusing finger at her. "It's our duty to slay her!" Several villagers pushed at her, ready to draw blood.

"No," said Pukuli. "Our duty is to protect the earth from demons!" Mukhiya looked around, shocked.

"Child, how dare you speak to me—"

"Pukuli is right," said the elder in white robes, who seldom spoke.

Villagers turned to him, amazed. "I've never heard his voice," murmured a youth. "I always thought he was mute," said another.

"We chose British coins over the safety of our people," said the silent elder. "We chose to shut our eyes, to ignore our problems, praying they'd go away." He pointed to Devi and spoke louder now. "But this brave woman has always put our welfare above her own. Even when it seems we're unworthy."

Arjuna looked on, ashamed.

The village elder raised a hand. "I am the hereditary Mukhiya of this village, as my father once was. And his father's father. And I say, no, she must die or be delivered to Mahisha."

"The real demon is among us," the silent elder responded. "And it's distrust and fear." Then, with a sidelong glance to Mukhiya, he added, "And even greed. All the Mukhiyas before you served the best interests of the village. So, too, must you."

Devi pressed her hands together and bowed gratefully, for even if she died at the hands of this mob, she no longer felt alone and misunderstood.

Finally, Arjuna spoke up above the motley crowd. "I'm ashamed, but I, too, put my own selfishness ahead of the village—ahead of Devi. There's no excuse for my behaviour. All I can do is apologize and try to make things right."

Devi was shocked by Arjuna's generous words and felt momentarily overwhelmed by emotion.

"I fought alongside her," continued Arjuna. "No one—no man or woman—is more brave, more capable of leading us. A Gurkha's true glory has never been in fighting. It's in our faith and our willingness to risk our lives for each other. For years, Mahisha has terrorized our village and so many others, and he'll do it again and again, whether we choose to defend ourselves or not. So let's fight shoulder-to-shoulder with Devi.

Devi herself remained unconvinced. "Back in the trenches, I was powerless to change the war. To change fate."

"But maybe here, now, with the blessing of Lord Krishna and the goddess, Devi, you can make a difference," said Arjuna.

Devi wasn't ready to be a leader, but she also knew she was being called upon to fulfill her duty, a duty she now understood Dharma had been preparing her for. "In the war, we saw how badly it went blindly following the orders of the British command. We need to wage our war another way," she said to the villagers.

"You are all rugged people, heroes of your own lives, of your own stories, who have made a life out of the tough soil and unpredictable mountains. You've made countless decisions about your survival and the survival of your families in the past, so I want you to rely on your knowledge and instinct, always keeping in mind our goal—to vanquish the demon."

The villagers moved toward Devi, as if being drawn by some magical force. At the same time, Colonel Young gave the command to the British and Welsh troops to withdraw from the square. They turned on their heels and abandoned the village.

All the elders, but for Mukhiya, bowed to Devi in affirmation.

The sad and frightened faces of villagers continued to stare back at her, and Devi understood what needed to happen, so she bowed to them, accepting the weight of her responsibility.

Only then did Mukhiya step forward, reluctantly joining Devi's army.

*

In view of Mahisha's kingdom where storm clouds of fire and smoke whirled above, Devi hiked up the hill and arrived before Dharma's hut. The fire had consumed so much. She sifted through the charred remains where only sections of the stone wall still stood. Dharma's photos with his wife had been turned to ash, as had all of Dharma's other earthly possessions. She tried not to mourn, remembering what Dharma had once told her. That the world of names and forms was always changing. They could be created and destroyed—unlike the infinite *Atman*, the eternal soul that pervaded everything, which was never born and never died.

Devi approached a blackened mound of hot ash, probing it with a foot. There, in the midst of all that debris, she uncovered the crisp, burnt fabric covering Dharma's kukri. She picked up the knife and marveled. The kukri glistened, untouched by the destruction around it. She looked up and caught sight of dozens of men gathered on the valley floor, as they saddled up their horses and strapped down bags.

*They're leaving!* she gasped.

Devi raced downhill, springing from terrace to terrace, defying gravity. By the time she had arrived by the river, the Welsh and British soldiers, including Colonel Young, had mounted their horses in preparation for their departure. Cadogan noticed something among their numbers and turned to the others, concerned. "Where's Maddocks?"

"Well hell if I know," answered Hardie. "And if he doesn't join us now, it'll be a long way back home for him all alone."

Devi grabbed hold of the harness of Hughes' horse to stop him from leaving.

The major gazed down on Devi, regretfully.

"We fought for you," she pleaded.

"A woman of all things!" wailed Smith. "Fighting with men! The shame of it!"

Colonel Young bristled in his saddle at the very thought of it.

"She fought more bravely than any of you," said Cadogan.

"Are you thinking about sticking around here to fight their fight?" retorted Smith. "You don't have a clue what you'd be fighting, do you?"

"I admit, I have many questions about the nature of the adversary," said Hughes, reluctantly.

The British and Welsh troops looked to each other, doubtful of their willingness to take up arms for the Nepalese.

Cadogan suddenly looked sure of himself and jumped off his horse. "Hey Manchester," he called out to Smith. "These hillmen—"

"*Ehm*, and hillwomen," corrected Hardie, eyeing Devi.

"These hill-people here fought and died in the mud for your empire of dung. And they'd do it again if ya asked. So if they're asking us to fight for their village or even their grandma's favourite tea pot, damn it, we fight! It's the least we can do."

Seeing Hughes step off his horse, the colonel pulled on his well-oiled moustache and cleared his throat. "Major," he said to Hughes. "I need not remind you we're not permitted to involve ourselves with internal matters."

"This is *our* hour of need," interjected Devi.

"I'm afraid I don't believe in demons," said Hughes.

"Well, that's a bloody good thing, Major," Young erupted. "Because any fool that believes in demons is an even bigger fool!"

"I don't believe in demons," repeated Hughes, looking to the colonel and then to Devi. "But I have faith in you."

Colonel Young spat in the dirt in disgust. "Are you disobeying my command?" he barked.

Suddenly, from the forest emerged Private Maddocks, his gun trained on the colonel. "*LONG NOSE!*" he shouted at Young.

The colonel turned to Hughes, livid. "Major! Put a leash on your stray Taff!"

"MADDOCKS!" shouted Hughes. "Have you gone mad!"

"I've lived with your secret long enough," Maddocks growled at Young. "The colonel here executed Anwyl. In cold blood. At point blank. No court-martial, no chance to defend himself, even."

"Are you sure?" asked Hughes.

"I saw it with my own eyes. On my family name, I swear it."

Young didn't protest. "Orders are bloody orders! Just like they are now!" he said, drawing his pistol on Maddocks, who remained steadfast, unmoved by the gun pointed at him.

"Stand down, Maddocks," commanded Hughes.

Maddocks didn't budge.

"Have it your way," said Young. And there and then, he shot Maddocks where he stood.

A gasp, as every soldier and officer present tried to make sense of what they had just witnessed. Hughes' cheeks flushed bright red, and he pulled his side piece on Young. Now all the Welsh and English aimed their guns at the colonel, including Young's most loyal servant.

"Even you Smith!" shouted Young.

Smith cocked his pistol, livid, ready to shoot. "Anwyl was an innocent lamb," he stammered, with uncharacteristic emotion. "He didn't deserve to die by your hand. And now Maddocks? You aren't a leader. You're a monster."

"Hold your fire, sergeant," barked Hughes. "We have enough witnesses to this murder to have this foul human court-marshalled."

Young faced dozens of pistols and rifles. Seeing he had no allies among the cowardly lot, he forced his horse backward in retreat toward the forest. "Traitors, one and all! I will have YOU court-martialed and hung by your filthy necks!"

"You'll get yours!" spat Cadogan, his face streaked with tears.

"We'll see about that, you dirty Welshman!" responded Young, fumbling his words. He quickly escaped into the thick of the woods.

*

Toward the edge of town, several villagers dressed in white wept before the funeral pyres, where smoke and flame rose to the heavens. Throughout the rest of the village, people moved about with a sense of fateful purpose. Some sat on their haunches sharpening their knives and swords. Others cleaned their guns and made arrows. An eager looking Tibetan mastiff was being fitted with body armour studded with large deadly spikes.

The British and Welsh worked together hauling large stones into place to fortify their positions where several cannons had already been mounted, aiming downhill. Several soldiers fixed their sword bayonets beneath their rifles, as they reminisced about Maddocks and his fierce loyalty and love of long-winded insults.

Nearby, a dejected looking Uruwasi passed Major Hughes, who smiled and bowed to her with palms pressed together. It was an unexpected encounter for her that somehow took the sting out of Arjuna's rejection. She returned the gesture, respectfully, and carried on her way.

In view of the mural of the supreme goddess, Devi, a villager tested the tension of his bow, while Birendra, dressed in fresh linens, examined the point of his kukri. Anish's mother measured the weight of a sword before making several expert strokes with it.

Soon dozens of men and women filed into the square on horseback, with deadly bows strung over their shoulders, their arrows sharpened and ready for battle.

"Women warriors," marvelled Pukuli, as she coiled a thick length of rope.

"Our village has a long history of female fighters. As it appears does yours," said one of the women on horseback, as she admired the women folk of the village preparing weapons.

"It's a new thing," admitted Pukuli.

"Well, hundreds more of our best archers await below," advised the woman on horseback. Word had apparently made its way up and down the surrounding valleys of the impending fight against the demon, who had caused so much destruction. Right behind the archers, several elephants fitted with large saddles and the *OM* symbol painted between their eyes arrived from the lower valley alongside hundreds more warriors. Dharma's village greeted each one as a hero.

Devi instructed the new arrivals to cut down the swinging rope bridge strung over the Kali Gandaki River to slow the demon army's advance. She approached a group of children and requested they make several different coloured kites.

"What for?" asked one.

"So you can talk to each other."

Their eyes lit up in comprehension. She bowed and left them to complete their work.

At the village forge, a man and woman worked the iron into weapons, hammering, sending sparks in all directions.

Devi joined Pukuli, who was tying one end of the long rope around a tree.

Badri sneered, as he watched them working. "You're tying it wrong! It'll never hold!"

Pukuli smiled, sprang through the air and landed before him. Expertly, she tossed her kukri back and forth between hands, putting on an impressive display of knife work. "It's okay," she said. "You've always looked for reasons to be unhappy. Perhaps you're just scared you won't measure up."

For a brief moment, Badri's arrogant expression fell with her words like a mask swiped from his narrow face. Then he stalked away to hide his shame.

Now some distance away, Colonel Young eased his pace, having made good progress. As he rode through the veil of darkness, he had to stay focused to find the path back to the British barracks above Pokhara and the malaria-infested shores of Lake Phewa. He needed to raise the alarm on the unforgiveable mutiny that had just taken place.

But strange noises erupted from the forest. He looked around. "Who's there?" he called, trying to keep the tremor of fear out of his voice.

Low growling from the forest.

All at once, a black mass sprang at him, knocking him to the ground. The sound of slow crunching bones and a deathly gasp.

The colonel, who had survived so many battles in Europe and Asia, and who, himself, had taken so many lives, drew his very last breath trapped beneath the pressing weight of an unearthly demon with rows of razor-sharp teeth and breath like sulphur.

*

Back at the plaza of Dharma's village, Arjuna bowed before the painting of the goddess Devi, his kerchief tied around his neck. He prayed first to Ganesh, the bringer of good luck, in the hopes that the elephant god could intervene, removing all obstacles in the village's path.

Holding a lotus flower, Devi kneeled beside him, her hand only a touch away from his. Their eyes met.

"Dharma had always been right about you," said Arjuna. "That you possessed something great. Perhaps for a time I was jealous that he saw it in you and not me."

Devi was about to speak, but Arjuna cut her off, kindly. "I'm at peace with this. And now we've finally arrived back at the place where we began before the war," said Arjuna. "Facing Mahisha."

"The same, but different," offered Devi.

"How so?"

"As a child, I saw life as a straight line, but now I see it as a cycle, like the seasons in all their variety from year to year."

Arjuna nodded in affirmation.

"Do you think we're ready? Can we win this time?"

"You already know, Arjuna. You saw it in the trenches. In war, there's no winning. Even in victory, a part of us will be lost forever."

Arjuna shook his head, plagued by so many questions. "You and I have lived through so much. But I've never been more confused as now. Why is this? I've spent my life trying to understand the nature of the immortal. My mind knows the universal soul is imperishable and that *moha*, my attachment to worldly things—including, I confess, you—is where my doubt lies," he stumbled.

Devi couldn't look away, as Arjuna spoke of what weighed on him so heavily, her soft eyes set on him.

"But enlightenment doesn't exist in the intellect or my physical senses," he continued. "And that scares me. I want to be free of suffering. I want to dwell in the oneness of the Brahmic state—for eternity."

His words tailed off, as he suffered with his doubts. "You're witness to my confusion, I'm afraid. But at least I accept that, too. Because I trust you with my life. So tell me, Devi, how can I know what's real?"

Devi touched her forehead. "Fate may be written here," she said, before touching Arjuna's chest. "But the truth lives here. Where no masks can be worn."

"Do you think our hearts can rewrite destiny?"

Devi rose and wordlessly offered him the flower.

He accepted it, before confessing: "Krishna teaches us that you can only kill the body. That the soul is immortal. But I'm still scared." He untied his beloved kerchief and presented it to Devi. She tied it around her neck, feeling as if Arjuna, himself, was now a part of her.

# SHARPENING THE SPEAR

Dharma's village appeared deserted in the faint glow of early morning. Across the valley, among the blackened mountains, stood Mahisha's kingdom, where storm clouds of fire and smoke boiled across the sky.

In the distance, the faint sound of a warped conch shell being blown delivered fear directly to the hearts of the villagers tucked away in their hiding spots. Among them, some prayed to the gods for protection. Others prayed for a quick and painless death.

From his place, kneeling among the tall grass, Arjuna responded to Mahisha's call to battle. He drew in a deep breath and blew into a divine conch brought back in an unknown time from a distant supernatural sea. The sound reassured the villagers—until the thunder of stampeding hoofs grew louder.

Soon Mahisha's hordes could be seen descending on the valley, blackening the earth like a plague. More fissures appeared in the earth, bubbling with red-hot magma.

Hundreds of monkey-faced demons with fangs and razor claws charged toward the river. Several tumbled into the fast-moving waters and were carried away on the current. Others came to a halt, uncertain how to proceed.

"Look," said a villager, from his hiding place. "Without the bridge, they can never make it across!"

No sooner had those words been spoken did hundreds of long-spined crocodile demons arrive at the bank of the river, forming a bridge across the turbulent water. The monkey-faced creatures scampered across the demonic bridge and headed uphill toward the village.

Then, from nowhere, Devi appeared on a mound above the valley, wearing combat boots and the fitted red dress that once belonged to Dharma's beloved wife. The pistol and kukri strapped to her waist gave her some measure of security, though she knew that weapons alone would not be enough in this battle.

128

Down below, the monkey demons bound up the terraces toward Dharma's village, hungry to destroy all that stood in their master's way.

Devi drew the kukri with the handle made from a piece of Ganesh's tusk, feelings its power in her grip. As she raised the curved knife high, a hundred flaming arrows arced across the sky as though the heavens themselves were raining fire.

In the distance, a dozen monkeys fell in a hail of arrows, popping like liquid-filled balloons.

Devi signaled to the children with the different coloured kites. "Send up the black ones," she commanded.

The kids, who were spread out across the village and terraces, sent their black kites skyward, and the ruins behind Devi came alive. Villagers emerged from rooftops and walls, from piles of rubble and bushes.

A group of village defenders gathered on a steep slope gave each other one last nervous glance before forcing out the wooden planks securing several large boulders in their place. Without the supporting wood, the mammoth rocks tore loose from the earth, and gravity did the rest.

Down below, several *asura* felt the earth rumbling and looked about, confounded, until the first boulder squashed one, followed by a second.

From their trench overlooking the valley, the British and Welsh saw the trees below swaying and the branches rattling—but they could see no adversaries. "Fire," called Hughes, anyway. As the artillery shells flashed across the sky and shattered into fragments on impact with the trees, the soldiers were already reloading more ammunition and propellant into the rear chamber of the barrel.

"Well, boys, this may be the strangest war we've ever fought," Hughes confessed to his men. "Godspeed, one and all."

"Godspeed," they responded in unison to their commanding officer.

Armed with an array of weapons, villagers of all ages charged from the ruins of the village on foot, horseback, and mounted on elephants.

"Ayo Gurkhali!" they hollered.

A monkey demon ran uphill but vanished into a concealed trap. Satisfied, an old villager looked down into the hole he had dug to see the *asura* wriggling on the buried spears. But another demon monkey sprang on him and latched onto his face, savagely biting and tearing. They both tumbled into the hole and sunk onto the fatal spears. "My destiny," the old man whispered with his last breath, hoping to reach the doors of nirvana with the transmigration of his soul.

As two demons rushed up hill, a villager with leaves attached to her clothing for camouflage leapt from behind a tree and swatted the creatures with her spade.

Along the terraces, the villagers speared and cut down the demon army, until, finally, the river valley fell silent.

Devi called to the others: "Recover your defensive positions!"

"Why?" a villager responded.

Devi pointed down the slope.

Thousands of undivine beings of all types—pig-faced with claws, six legged creatures with hoofed feet, wild boars with red fiery eyes—clamoured up the lower terraces like a grim infestation.

Devi jumped on her horse and galloped downhill towards the fast-approaching army.

The two sides crashed together with the force of opposing oceans, sending up clouds of dust, shields, and spears.

Devi's horse charged forward, leaping down the terraces. Three demoniacal creatures spotted her and hurled long spears. The sharp points pierced her horse. With a horrible neigh, the horse crumpled, catapulting Devi, who rolled across the ground. But she came to a rest on her feet, crouched low in a battle-ready position, kukri in hand.

The legs of horses and elephants moved dangerously around her, threatening to trample her. "Don't let them into the village!" she implored the others.

A boy defending the village entrance with a club spiked with nails was cut down by a horde of Mahisha's underlings. His mother huddled over his lifeless body, weeping. Then, with resolve, she picked up his weapon and went in pursuit of the ungodly monsters.

Devi was quickly surrounded by a dozen grotesque beasts armed with spears and swords. In a blur of motion, she pulled a spear from the hand of a minion and used it to peg its clawed foot to the ground. She sprang onto its head, ran over the others like stepping stones, then whirled to the ground.

A demon attempted to penetrate her defenses but was dealt a crushing blow.

Another creature attacked but was kicked hard, bowling over other beasts from the demon underworld.

Rakesh pressed against a stone wall, one eye peering out at the pitch battle. "How much longer?" he asked himself, impatiently.

The British and Welsh soldiers looked out on the battlefield before them, bewildered. What they saw were the villagers engaged in combat with invisible foes.

A villager stumbled in front of the British trench, in the grip of mortal combat with an unseen enemy.

As Hardie gripped his rifle with the mounted bayonet at the ready, he called out, "What should we do?"

"Shoot!" commanded Hughes. "Just in front! But do avoid the villager!"

British guns opened fire in a hail of bullets and smoke.

There was a shrill beastly squeal from a wounded—unseen—demon. The soldiers looked to each other in disbelief. The villager escaped, grateful for the help.

The British and Welsh soldiers watched with mouths agape, as the monster faded into view on the ground. At that instant, Major Hughes looked out at the battlefield. His eyes grew wide. The invisible demons attacking the villagers suddenly became visible. The others looked out at the battlefield. They all went wide-eyed, too.

Just then, several beasts with jagged breastbones broke through the line of British and Welsh rifles. They trounced the soldiers, slicing them with their sharp keels of bone.

The demons worked with savage speed, mauling Sergeant Smith with their razor teeth, ripping at his flesh, his horrified screeches haunting the British trench. From his back pocket, Smith managed to pull out the metal comb reserved for his precious hair and used it to stab the creatures over and over again—but to little effect.

Major Hughes fumbled to reload his pistol and shot the hideous brutes off Smith, one by one. *Pop! Pop! Pop!* Smith gasped and ripped the limp creatures off him then looked to Hughes. He pressed his palms together, bowing to his commander.

A brief nod from Hughes. "Now pick up your gun, sergeant, and keep firing!"

An elephant ridden by the quiet elder in white robes trampled a group of Mahisha's brutes, while a pack of Tibetan mastiffs with their spiked suits of armour charged at another group of demons.

Flaming arrows streaked overhead in both directions on their way to meet unseen foes. Arrows collided in mid-air, splintering down on the invading army.

All around, villagers were engaged in fierce hand-to-hand combat, striking the beasts with fists and elbows, knees and feet, and knives and lances. Another villager fell victim to the vicious onslaught by Mahisha's demons. It was a battle to the death, and every villager knew it.

As Devi fought, she looked up and witnessed young Anish, with cheeks puffed and a flaming stick in hand, as he sprayed rice wine from his mouth, blowing a fire ball of flame. A beast darted away on fire, screeching.

Pukuli battled monsters with two kukris, her knives dancing like fireflies. She stepped aside, revealing Badri, who gladly fought alongside this brave girl.

"You were training hard while we were away!" said Badri.

At the river below, Arjuna fought three attackers at once, cutting and warding them off. A fourth one leapt on his back, holding a blade made of bone at his throat.

As Birendra grappled another beast, he saw Arjuna in trouble. He quickly dispatched the wicked thing in his grips and moved up behind Arjuna, tearing the minion off.

In the village, Mahisha's army breached the defenses and poured in through the gap. One of the soulless underlings threw a flaming stick inside a house, igniting the building. A foot greeted the creature, sending it inside the burning house.

A group of children saw demon boars with fiery red eyes and razor-sharp tusks stampede toward them. The kids took off in two different directions, hoping the invading hordes would take chase. The kids weaved their way through the narrow streets just ahead of the dripping snouts and deadly tusks of the wild boars. Now the two groups of children rounded a corner and were running right at each other.

"Ayo!" the kids called to each other, as they leapt out of the way, allowing the two waves of pursuing demon boars to smash into each other's pointed tusks. The horrible squeals of dying boars rose over the village, momentarily hushing the warring parties on the battlefield.

Not far away, in between the narrow rows of stone houses, Rakesh hopped as fast as he could on one leg, as he was chased through the labyrinth of laneways he knew so well. At the last second, he jumped a wide leather strap laid out on the ground. The creatures stepped on it, triggering a series of deadly poison darts that flew through the window, striking them down. Rakesh only had a second to rejoice before several more beasts sprang on him.

Devi came upon Rakesh as he battled Mahisha's demons with heart and soul. She watched as another beast attacked from his flank, but Badri was there and hurled a pitchfork, trapping the foul demon in its prongs.

Devi, Rakesh, and Pukuli saluted Badri for his efforts, and for the first time in his life he felt in his chest the tremendous joy of belonging to something greater than himself.

"We are warriors," said Badri, soberly. "And perhaps we've always been destined to die on the battlefield."

"But hopefully not today!" offered Rakesh.

With so much fighting left to be done, they hastily scattered in all directions.

For miles around, hundreds of battles were unfolding between villagers and Mahisha's army. It was sword against knife. Arrows against rifles. Villagers fought ferociously, some riding horses and elephants. A monster attacked Pukuli's mother, who speared the supernatural thing and left it to languish on the pole.

Bodies from both sides littered the battlefield.

Devi looked up from her place among the battling villagers only to see a murmuration of flying beasts swoop and swirl high overhead, each fixed with a sharpened bony appendage that served as a deadly lance. The dark twisting shapes created by the flying horde were mesmerizing, and their countless numbers nearly blotted out the sky.

Several flying demons broke from the black shape-shifting cloud and swung into a roaring dive, zooming toward the villagers below.

All expression drained from Devi's face.

As a farmer combated a pig-faced brute using his shovel as a shield, a flying beast dove at him from behind. A jolt ran through his body, and he looked down at his hands wrapped around the bone piercing his belly. The bone weapon withdrew, leaving a gaping hole, before he collapsed.

All around, villagers fell in growing numbers to the flying beasts.

One of the flying abominations aimed its bony lance at Devi. She rolled out of the way just in time, wrapping a rope around its deadly appendage. It flew on.

The coil of rope quickly unraveled with one end tied to a tree. The rope grew taut, and the flying creature sling-shotted hard to the ground, where Devi finished it off. But its flesh grew around the weapon, trapping her. She tried to withdraw the knife, but it wouldn't budge. The demon's flesh creeped up her arm, threatening to encase her in its deathly ooze. With a brutal twist of the kukri, she sliced her way out.

Nearby, Major Hughes pointed to the skies. "Aim high!" he commanded his men.

The troops fired volley after volley at the flying beasts, as they dive bombed their positions.

A British soldier met the spear point of a demon and was carried off.

Far above the valley, the British soldier wriggled on the skewer point of the flying beast, until he was released and plummeted, shrieking, to his end.

In the distance, a fresh wave of demons attacked, then another. It seemed Mahisha had an endless supply of reinforcements for his army. Their numbers soon overwhelmed the battlefield, sending a wave of panic and back and forth shouting among the villagers.

Devi wasn't blind to the situation. For every villager that remained stood a hundred or more devilish creatures hungry for battle. And she was not deaf to the horrible cries of pain and coming death from her people, who lay like broken sticks scattered over the field of battle. This wasn't the time to think like a child, she admonished herself, to hope that everything would work out for Dharma's village or any of the other villages in the valley.

She called to the children with the kites: "FLY THE WHITE ONES!"

"No," cried a child. "It can't be over already!"

"DO IT!" Devi hollered.

One after the other, the white kites took flight, swooshing back and forth across the sky, and the villagers knew to fall back on the village.

Arjuna watched the arriving hordes, powerless. He begged the heavens in a choked voice: "Lord Krishna, please broker peace between our village and Mahisha's army."

Standing in full view on the hillside, Devi surveyed the river valley. Countless beasts surrounded the village. From the stillness of the mountains, warped wedding music reached her ears.

The villagers crouched defensively, their spears bristling outward. Mahisha's army did not push forward, in no hurry to challenge the points of their spears. Mahisha, with a garland of skulls around his neck, sat in a giant basket woven from blackened bones. His servants struggled under the weight of the basket, as they carried him uphill toward the town plaza.

Several servants danced and played off-key music on instruments carved from human bones.

The wedding party flanked by Mahisha's serpent royal guards arrived before the rattling spears of the villagers.

From behind the wall of lances stepped Major Hughes. He walked directly up to Mahisha and fired his pistol.

The bullets had no effect.

The demon swiped at Hughes, sending him back painfully against the spears.

Injured but conscious, Hughes was hauled away by his men, his smashed glasses crooked on his face.

*

The injured were tended to by the villagers, including Major Hughes, whose wounds were gently cleaned by Uruwasi.

"*Diolch cariad*," he said in Welsh.

"What does that mean?" asked Uruwasi.

"It's a term of endearment," he responded, shyly. "It means, *Thank you, dear*."

Together, they smiled and blushed.

Pukuli, Arjuna, and Rakesh followed Devi across the plaza, until she came to an abrupt halt. She removed her combat boots so that she was barefoot. Then she unbuckled her holster. She handed her possessions to Pukuli and was left only with Dharma's kukri at her waist.

Devi signaled for everyone to move back.

"But we can still take him *together*!" said Rakesh.

"You're already with me," responded Devi, touching her chest above her beating heart.

Mahisha entered the plaza in the giant basket, surveying the scene with satisfaction. "Ah, my bride," he said, gazing upon Devi.

The demon's oxen muscles glistened, his horns razor sharp.

Silence swept over the village, as few had ever seen Mahisha up close. He was large, twice the size of the largest beasts of burden in the valley. His acrid scent was that of burnt meat left too long on the fire.

Rakesh hopped back toward the plaza entrance, while Arjuna stayed by Devi's side.

For a precious moment, Arjuna and Devi pressed their foreheads together. "I had truly believed that Lord Krishna or the goddess Devi would save us from this," he said, despondent.

"Have faith," said Devi.

Now Arjuna was forced back by Birendra.

With a kindly hand, Devi prompted Pukuli to move away, but the girl stood defiantly between Devi and the *asura*.

Pukuli's mother looked fearfully from the hillside at the central plaza below.

Devi was now face to face with Pukuli. "You're very brave. The bravest of the brave."

Mahisha's shadow moved over Devi and Pukuli, stealing the light around them.

Devi continued to focus on Pukuli. "But it's your mother who needs you now."

Pukuli reached for Devi's hand, who steered her clear, just as Mahisha arrived before her. "My queen," he said. "There's no need for all this drama!"

Devi's hand hovered over the kukri in its scabbard.

Mahisha beckoned her into the matrimonial basket. "Come. You've done enough harm to these unfortunate people."

Devi took in the situation: The demon. Birendra and one-legged Rakesh struggling to hold Arjuna back. The regretful look of villagers and British and Welsh troops alike.

Rising beyond the plaza were the blackened summits of Mahisha's formidable kingdom.

Finally, Devi spoke: "Take me to the mountain."

# LIVING THE DYING DREAM

Blood flowed through the cracks in the stone floor of the courtyard at the centre of Mahisha's castle, while human and animal body parts were sandwiched between the stacks of flat rocks in the walls, mortar for the demon's empire of terror. The yard smelled distinctly of iron and sulphur from the deepest recesses of the earth.

At the centre of the courtyard, a dark mercurial moat encircled a stone platform where Devi and Mahisha now stood. A half-formed demon dog took shape in the liquid womb then clawed its way out and shook itself off, sending drops of acid sizzling on the floor.

Above the platform, the roofless courtyard opened up to the clouds.

Mahisha stared upwards and recognized how close he now was to the heavens. He was so close, he could almost taste the gods, he marveled. The end for them was really only the beginning for him.

Devi touched the surface of the moat that seemed devoid of light and life and examined her finger. It was the colour of blood. The glass-like surface of the pool broke into tiny ripples with a drip-drip-drip. Devi looked up to see animals—pigs, dogs, cats, buffalo—hung from wires, feeding the pool with their life force.

"Where's the priest?" bellowed the demon. "I want his blessing!"

"And fetch everyone from the village—to witness history," called Devi. "And have them bring libations. Of pure rice wine."

Mahisha looked impatiently toward his servants. "Do as my queen commands!"

Some time later, off-kilter wedding music played. On the other side of the moat from Mahisha and Devi, the surviving villagers gathered alongside the British and Welsh troops, holding cups and bottles.

Arjuna regarded the moat with grave concern. "I always understood the underworld to be *Patala*," he spoke softly to himself. "A sub-

139

terranean heaven filled with splendid jewels and seducing *asura* maidens. But I see only darkness here."

Mahisha gazed out at the scene, satisfied. Immortality was a very fine gift, he thought. And soon it would be his.

As a small token of gratitude, Mahisha presented Devi with her father's rusted kukri, the one Dharma had used to unsuccessfully end Mahisha's reign, while she was off fighting in the trenches of Europe.

Devi's welling anger at the sight of the knife and all that had been lost took Mahisha by surprise. But then he grew amused. The demon was still human enough to recognize it would take the girl some time to adjust to her new reality.

Then Arjuna's shadow flew across the room.

"Devi!" he shouted.

Mahisha frowned at the presence of this irritation and watched as Arjuna bowed to Devi, humbly. "I owe you my life, but all I can offer you is this," he said, tapping his chest.

Without hesitation, Mahisha swatted Arjuna. His neck snapped with a terrible crack, as he flew across the moat and into the wall. Several horrified villagers rushed to Arjuna's side to tend to his mortal wounds.

Mahisha grinned at Devi, who shook with fists clenched. The sound of moaning stole her attention.

Devi clutched Dharma's kukri in its scabbard and looked for the source of the sorrowful groans.

"Ah, do you hear them?" said Mahisha. "Your mother? Your father? And, of course, my beloved father, Dharma."

"He could never have created such a monster!" she growled.

"You're wrong," he said, defiantly. "Dharma took me in after my parents died. Just like you."

Elbows, hands, and faces now pressed from inside Mahisha's flesh, the lost souls trapped within.

In the near distance, Arjuna remained motionless on the ground.

It was all too much for Devi. She was still not free of the mental fever burning inside, her pain driving her to action. She drew the kukri strapped to her waist.

"Marry me, or the same fate awaits all of them," said Mahisha, pointing a claw at the villagers on the far side of the moat.

Devi launched a frenzied attack. She chopped and hacked him, but somehow his muscles grew bigger with each strike. He shape-shifted—from buffalo to tiger, tiger to rhino.

Above the courtyard, dark clouds sped across the early morning sky.

Devi moved like a woman possessed. Mahisha seemed thrilled doing battle with his bride to be, as if it were all just a game. "You're going to wear yourself out for our wedding night!"

The demon sprang at Devi, snorting and bellowing, before transforming through his mouth into an elephant.

Devi recoiled at the abominable sight of his metamorphosis.

The elephant charged, and Devi fell beneath its trampling legs.

Mahisha spun around, only to find Devi lifeless on the ground. The *asura* rose on hind legs like a stallion and charged toward Devi, his tusks bent low.

As the tusks were about to gore her, she rolled clear of the depression in the floor, and the demon's tusks pierced the ground. Mahisha, by his own force, stopped dead, head twisting, his massive weight airborne.

Rakesh looked on in horror. "Watch out!"

Devi sprang clear of Mahisha's earth-trembling crash.

With a swift motion of her blade, Devi cut off the elephant's trunk.

The demon did not move.

Major Hughes, bandaged but still bleeding, adjusted his badly twisted glasses, trying to confirm he had seen what he thought he had seen.

Devi turned to the villagers, chest heaving, feeling victorious.

Mahisha, shifting into a thorny-fleshed bear, rose up behind her and struck her to the ground. He hit her again, for good measure. After all, how could he tolerate such abuse from his own wife?

Bleeding profusely, Devi glanced at the trench encircling them. "Libations!"

The villagers remained absolutely still, uncertain of the command.

But Anish, the youth firebreather, understood right away. "Pour rice wine! Into the moat!"

Despite their confusion, the villagers, along with the British and Welsh, did as the child directed and poured their cups and bottles into the moat.

Mahisha seemed puzzled by the gesture but saw no threat. Until Devi struck her kukri against the stone – sending sparks flying.

The moat came alive with flames, and a wall of fire rose up around Devi and the demon.

Mahisha backed away from the flame, because although his world raged with fire, he himself was of the flesh, a flesh that burned.

Brandishing her kukri, Devi struck the demon over and over again with all the fury in her soul. She dove beneath Mahisha and kicked his feet out from beneath him. He landed hard, rattling the earth. But, still, Mahisha rose up, undefeated. He swung at Devi with the force of ten kicking horses.

The onlookers groaned in sympathy.

Devi lay battered in the cage of fire, as Mahisha approached. "Our journeys in this world are not unlike," the demon uttered, almost sympathetically. "Outsiders who've never really been accepted by anyone. But my escape from *samsara*, from this ghastly cycle of birth, death, and rebirth, will not end with nirvana." A smile played across his lips. "Join me, and we'll build an immortal kingdom."

"Such a frightened creature. Trying to be something you're not."

Angry smoke escaped Mahisha's nostrils, and he swung around and donkey-kicked her.

Devi hurtled through the flame into the fortress wall, leaving a large impression in the wall.

She slid to the ground, gasping, blood seeping from her mouth. There was fear in her eyes now, as the room faded in and out of focus. She saw Arjuna and crawled to his side. His breathing was shallow, barely a whisper.

He reached for Devi and clasped her hand. "Revenge won't bring them back."

"Save your energy, Arjuna."

"If only I had known the truth sooner," he said, his voice weak.

With those words, Arjuna relaxed in death.

"Come now," said Mahisha. "The wise don't grieve the living or dead. That's what Dharma used to say. He eyed the deadly wall of flame that trapped him in place.

Devi looked up, defeated. "Why me?" she pleaded.

"A goddess in all ways but one. Awareness of your true nature."

Devi was confounded.

"Yes, my bride! Yes! You are a goddess. And I need one to become a true immortal. With you by my side, we will go to war with the gods. And we will vanquish them! Then we will become the rulers of earth and heaven!" he said, triumphantly.

The demon eyed the villagers, suspiciously. "And all will worship *ME*. Anyone caught praying to any other god will die a thousand painful deaths. And why would they pray to dead gods, which they will all be, including the Supreme, Brahman!"

"I'm no goddess," said Devi. "And you are no god." Then, without judgment, she asked, "How did you lose yourself so completely? Love has no limits. But your hunger for power. Where does it end?"

As Devi rose to her feet, she heard Dharma speak: *Embrace him like someone you love.* She saw her mother smiling, and a smile returned to her lips.

The demon, still trapped in the cage of fire, seemed unsettled by her smile, as if she knew something he did not.

Devi stared at the knife in her hand.

*Nishkama Karma*, she remembered Arjuna once saying. *Acting without desire.*

In the stillness of her mind, body, and soul, there was one place yet for her to experience—beyond the straight lines and even the cycles of life, beyond the harmonizing paths of action, emotion, and intellect, a place infinite and unbroken.

She slid the kukri into its sheath and slipped off the belt with the dagger.

The *asura* grinned, relieved that the girl had finally surrendered to his will, while the villagers looked to one another, bewildered.

The bald sun began to rise into the clouded heavens.

Devi sprang through the flame onto the demon's back, barefoot and without weapons. She closed her eyes and saw with her mind the moment Mahisha had transformed into an elephant through the rhino's mouth.

Mounted on the demon's back, Devi remained as calm as the Buddha himself. "Is there still a *boy* inside the demon?"

Devi wrapped her arms and feet around Mahisha's neck, and, for an instant, it appeared she had ten arms. The demon's blood-shot eyes narrowed with incomprehension.

Major Hughes and the others watched, mouths agape.

Mahisha's underlings grew restless, but now the villagers seized the opportunity and drew the weapons they'd concealed in the sleeves of their shirts and beneath their heavy skirts, holding back the vile creatures with the points of their kukris and spears.

Mahisha, in the form of a bear, struggled to throw Devi off, choking.

Devi effortlessly stayed with him. "Embrace who you are. Not what you thought you needed to become."

For countless minutes, the demon struggled to free himself, while Devi's eyes remained as placid as still water. She no longer thought about the outcome of their battle—only her singular duty as a warrior to protect the earth from demons.

Then Mahisha's human form—a mere boy, thin, wet, and ghostly pale—slowly emerged from the mouth of the bear.

He slipped to the ground like a newborn calf.

Wearily, he spotted something on the floor. It was the inscription on Devi's blade: *TO MY CHILD. FORGED WITH THE LOVE OF A FATHER.*

Mahisha, the child, looked up with something approaching comprehension.

Devi gazed down on the boy, who now rested his head on the ground. His eyes closed, relieved. He could sleep now.

Mahisha's musicians dropped their instruments of bone, which shattered like glass.

Flames grew around Mahisha—the beastly shell of the demon—sending a funnel of fire toward the heavens.

The earth trembled. The fiery moat bubbled.

Those gathered looked to each other for answers until a sound like a giant breath stole their attention, and the demoniacal moat suddenly drained. The vacuum yanked the beasts' weapons from their clutches and sucked them into the belly of the earth. Some creatures clawed the stone but were dragged into the void of blackness.

The villagers panicked, fighting the force drawing them toward the precipice.

Devi gazed at the sky. "Help them," she pleaded.

Rakesh was dragged toward the edge, but Badri grabbed him just in time. He struggled to hold him in place, as he, too, was pulled toward the bottomless moat to the underworld.

Devi pleaded again to the heavens.

The blue God, Shiva, appeared as a ghostly presence. He took hold of Badri's slender but powerful arm, drawing the mortals away from the abyss.

More gods appeared like shadows—Krishna, Ganesh, Vishnu, Sarasvati, and Dhanwantari—protectively wrapping themselves around the villagers and the Welsh and British troops.

Across the vast river valley, Mahisha's demonic henchmen raised their shields against the tempest. Thousands of beasts were dragged toward Mahisha's kingdom only to be drawn back inside the elemental earth where they belonged.

Inside Mahisha's castle, Devi glowed like a lantern, a halo of light around her head. She looked up at the rising flames where the apparition of Arjuna's brother, Tej, rose toward the heavens. Arjuna's father followed. Then her own father rose up in the smoke and fire. Devi reached for him. He pressed his hands to her, in gratitude. At last, he was free from the belly of the beast.

Next, Dharma rose up, holding the hand of a woman. Devi's heart burst with joy seeing Dharma at last reunited with his beloved wife. Devi whispered a blessing for their eternal love.

The spirit of Arjuna soon journeyed upward, and Devi reached out desperately to hold him in place. She still had earthly attachments that she was not yet ready to let go of. But her efforts did no good, and Arjuna kept rising. The pain and pleasure of her life were woven together into a single tapestry.

She looked down where Mahisha's body once lay and saw that he had become a lotus flower. She picked it up, took hold of the magical kukri, and bowed over Arjuna's body. She placed the kukri in his hand. "Breathe!" she begged. But the spirit of Arjuna continued its journey upward, and his human form remained motionless on the ground.

Devi looked back to the heavens. "If this kukri is really magic, bring him back to life!"

But the magical kukri tumbled from Arjuna's lifeless hand. Her stiffened posture broke.

In the veil of flame consuming the fortress, Devi held the lotus and the kukri. She didn't see the apparition of her mother behind her. Devi's eyes grew glossy, and a single great tear welled up.

Her mother spoke: "Never hide your tears. They contain all the love and healing in the world." She kissed Devi's head before ascending.

The tear took form and rolled down her cheek. For an eternity, it hung off her chin, then fell through space, landing on Arjuna's lifeless cheek.

Up above, the light of the sacred fire reached the heavens.

Devi didn't see that Arjuna's soul descended from above and re-entered his bodily form. The glaze in his eyes lifted, and he stirred, managing a drowsy smile.

In the flames, Arjuna stood before Devi. They embraced, gazing at one another, their mouths almost touching.

They kissed. And with that kiss, the walls of her life collapsed like the house of her dreams swept away by a tremendous landslide. The revelation wiped away everything earthly she had known and loved—her parents, Dharma, the Himalayas, and, of course, Arjuna. And what lay beyond was *Atman*, pure consciousness, eternal, unbroken, all-seeing. And she felt God reside in her heart.

The wind started to blow. Light particles, like embers from a fire, whirled around them.

At once, what had been hidden was revealed: the many arms of the supreme goddess, Devi.

Arjuna was in awe of her cosmic form, but there was no fear, no feeling of being overwhelmed by the totality of her divine presence.

In her left hand, she carried the magical kukri. In her right hand, the closed lotus of Mahisha.

The villagers—men, women, and children—bowed to Devi in wonderment. Uruwasi stood near Major Hughes, and, together, they pressed their hands together in deep reverence.

Pukuli approached the funnel of flame, and through the wall of fire, Devi presented Pukuli with Dharma's mysterious kukri knife.

Devi surrendered her body to the earth like a snake shedding its skin, her physical form collapsing to the ground, separated forever from her soul. With her transformation complete, she drew Arjuna into her embrace, and they rose together on the smoke and flame, a magic glow surrounding them.

The shadow over Dharma's valley slowly lifted, revealing a fertile land reborn.

As the light grew more intense around Devi and Arjuna, she had a vision of colourful kites darting back and forth across the sky above Dharma's village, while down below adults and children hauled baskets filled with the harvest. Devi saw Uruwasi very pregnant gazing toward Hughes, who was wearing village linens. Badri carried a bundle of firewood on his head and stopped to bow respectfully at the painting of the goddess Devi riding the back of a tiger.

In a corner of the square, the elders sat with several older women and some younger members of the community, discussing something intently. And there was Pukuli in a shaman's mask surrounded by little boys and girls, as she displayed Dharma's magical kukri. "Our people are like this blade. Forged by the gods, we must always remain sharp and true."

Then Pukuli removed the mask and pointed to her chest. "And guided by compassion, we must never forget where demons lurk, waiting."

The kids sprang to their feet. "Ayo Gurkhali!"

Away in the distance, their cheers echoed through the valleys all the way to the snow-blown summits of the Himalayas.

"Ayo Gurkhali!" the mountains seemed to call.

Devi smiled one last time at the earthly world below and continued to rise with Arjuna until the blinding light had washed away everything, and there was only light.

# About the Author

Robert J. Brodey is an adventure travel writer, photographer, and an avid trail runner. He has spent much of his life exploring the world, including several memorable trips to Nepal in 2006 and 2008. His work has been published in numerous national and international publications, including The *Houston Chronicle, Toronto Star, Globe and Mail, Outpost Magazine*, and Costa Rica's *Adrenaline Factor* magazine. His first novel, *Josef's Lair*, is an epic Nazi-hunting thriller that spans the globe and explores the powerful forces that shape human history. His follow up novel, *The Long Run*, is a wilderness thriller set in British Columbia [both books are available in paperback and ebook]. He lives in Toronto, Canada, with his wife and son.

You can find him online here:

> **Instagram**: @cloudgazer.canada

> **Bluesky**: @RobertBrodey.bsky.social

> Visit his websites here: www.cloudgazer.com[1] and www.vicarious-traveller.com[2]

---

1. http://www.cloudgazer.com

2. http://www.vicarious-traveller.com

# Disclaimer

Despite the long list of wonderful and knowledgeable people who have read and commented on this story along its 21-year journey—first as a screenplay then as a novel—I remain solely responsible for any and all creative and historical oversights.

Although many of the events depicted in this novel surrounding the Gurkhas and their historical place in British conflicts are based on documented facts, I've taken a great deal of creative license to make space for the mythical and magical.

# Acknowledgements

Quite literally, this story would not exist without Michael Carter, Bob Thompson, and Romelle Espiritu, who were instrumental in its development as an animated screenplay from 2004 onward. Michael not only supported the film project, organizing a greenscreen photoshoot to help sell the vision, but it was also his idea and finances that put into motion our first trip to Nepal in 2006, which introduced us to the likes of Biren Gurung, a talented architect with many relatives who served as Gurkha soldiers in the British military. Our two trips to the Himalayas also brought us into the orbit of Khusbu Sakkar Shrestha, Sameena Shrestha, and Suyogya Man Tuladhar, among others (and the wonderful Gabi Laszinger, the founder of the orphanage Happy Children of e.V.).

With such a long timeline for the story's evolution, I regretfully can't recall everyone I coaxed into reading the original screenplay (for that I apologize). But certainly, the earlier readers include Michael Carter, Bob Thompson, Fred Fuchs, Susie Grondin, Leah Jaunzems, Cash Lim, Matt Taylor, Deborah Brodey, Lara Arabian, and Riley Adams. Romelle Espiritu also provided a great deal of the artwork during the visualization phase of the project, as well as the *Thanka* treatment of the book cover graphic (note: the project didn't make it to the big screen at the time of publication).

The final incarnation of *Gurkha* as a novel passed through the hands of Andrea Brodey, Romelle Espiritu, Michelle Gibbs, Lara Arabian, Tina Cheng, Karen Mondok, Andrea Grant, Simon Cotter, Deborah Brodey, Patricia Brodey, Tavia del Águila, Nick Gazda, Selia Karsten, and Biren Gurung, who diligently responded to all my odd cultural questions—even with the 10-hour time difference. *Gratitude!* A big thank you to *Helo Blod* and Sarah Salter (for their help with Welsh translations). A special acknowledgement to the Welsh actor Michael Sheen and his inspired speech to the Welsh football team before the World Cup (2022), which I used as a blueprint for Captain Hughes' speech to his men before battle.

Peace & love to my wife, Lara, and son, Sevan, and to my endlessly supportive mom and sibs: Michelle, Andrea, Deborah, and Simon. To Simon Reetham-Clayton, Trudy, my nieces and nephews, Quinn, Jaime, Michael, Emilia, and Alexander.

To my extended family of Brodeys, Peppers, and Roberts, as well as my vast Armenian family, including Lena, Maro, and Jiro Arabian, Araxie Robertson, Alex & Myriam, Sean & Sarika, and the rest of the family in Toronto, L.A., Lebanon, and Syria.

To John Hatton, who left us in 2023 at the age of 91. He was a wise and wildly interesting man, with a keen sense of fairness and a tremendous curiosity for the world. He also had a contagious laugh unique to this world. And to his beloved Pat Hatton, who continues to inspire me during our weekly calls.

I also dedicate this book to that great swath of family and friends that have populated my life from my earliest years, including the Verbas, Chris and Jonathan Fitzpatrick, France Simard & Susan Lee, Riley Adams & Leslie Parker, Gary Gibbs and the good people at GibbsLaw LLP, Naomi & Jason Robinson, Kevin Allen & Andrea Brockie, Jordan Cheskes & Sam Sherkin (& Wills and Johnny Lee), Kumail Karimjee & Sarah Elton, Ivy Lim-Carter, Everton Wallace & Katherine Parris, Wudasie Efrem & Dereje Demissie, Mahitab & Arin (and the kids!), Karen & Brett Mondok, Annie Mandlsohn, Leah Jaunzems & Claire Harvey, Scott Enns & Paula Devonshire, Marlisa Budihardjo, Alarice Jones, Kim Li, Pui Sim, Lily Ng, Sarah Kurita, Lisa Forman, Aviva Chernick, Noelle Sadinsky, Alanna Marshall and the extensive Jarvis posse, the Joneidi sisters, Andrea Grant, Andrew Alzner, Ingrid Jones & Thomas Bollmann, Fabiola Bassong, Boza & Peter Sperr, Kara & Guillermo Del Aguila, Patty & Andrés Berger, Mitsuo and Kevin, Anurita Bains, Andrew Wanjohi, Chris Peake & Sylvie Duong, Anne Appathurai, Veena Verma & Pierre Brun, my Zumbado family in Costa Rica, Rodrigo Moreno & Diane, and Rosa Mesa & Thomas Proffe. A special shout out to Paul Shuper & Cindy Trayling, Tina Cheng & Brent Berry, Noura Kevorkian & Paul Scherzer, Paul Drumonde & Luana DiCandia, Troy Young & Lisa Nikifork Young, Gregor Kranjc & Jessica Campbell-Rogers, Niara Modi & Gerald Matlofsky, Luis & Luisa Martinez, Salima Pirani, and Riccardo Di Sipio & Elena Ferranti.

Big thank you to Löys and Alison Maingon, who opened their doors to me on Vancouver Island in 2024, took me for long walks in the mountains, fed me, discussed life, and gave me the space to work on this book.

Finally, a special dedication to Michael Verba, who died of cancer way too young in the fall of 2023. His support of my writing always blew me away. Just one month before he died, his health failing, he posted a review of my second novel, *The Long Run*. It was a staggering act of kindness, love, and support. I will always miss him. To his wife, Nancy, and daughter, Maddie, the Brodeys will always be your second family.

Given there are so many other wonderful people in my life, I will have to save some trees and take solace that you know who you are.